M000233658

Tuna Tango

Will Service Adventures

Steven Becker

Copyright © 2014 by Steven Becker
All rights reserved.
No part of this book may be reproduced in any form or by any
electronic or mechanical means, including information storage and
retrieval systems, without written permission from the author,
except for the use of brief quotations in a book review.

* * *

Join my mailing list
and get a free copy of Wood's Ledge
http://mactravisbooks.com

Chapter 1

Will looked down at the pale green water, reached around, pulled the five-pound anchor from the cooler behind him and dropped it into the water so as not to upset the balance of the stand-up paddle board. "Here." He tossed a line to Sheryl, paddling next to him. She caught it and tied a half-hitch to the crate strapped to the front of her board. Connected, the couple exchanged smiles.

"So far so good," she said as she reached for the spinning rod and picked it out of the foot-long length of PVC pipe strapped to the crate. Will had already rigged an artificial shrimp to the end of the line, with several small split-shot weights several feet above.

"Right there." He pointed with the confidence of someone who spent years of his life on the water. "The oyster bar goes to sand along that line." He made a motion with his hand, showing the direction of the bar so that she knew where to cast. He'd been doing the same for last fifteen years in the crystal clear waters of the Florida Keys, showing clients exactly where to pull out the trophy bonefish, permit, and tarpon. The murky waters of Tampa Bay were a challenge for sight fishing, but the bay offered great fishing. And that made it worthwhile. That and as much as he would have liked to be another four degrees of latitude south, that door had closed for now.

She cast the lure at the spot he had pointed to, let the small weight take it to the bottom, and closed the bail. "Now what?"

"Just bring it in a little at a time. Jiggle the rod to give it some life. You should have a hit shortly."

He had been careful when planning this outing. The truth was, it was more of a business presentation than a fishing trip. Her buy-in to his latest idea was essential. After the hurricane that had torn through the lower Keys the summer before had wiped him out, and his only assets, a flats boat and an unfinished house—both uninsured, were lost to the storm. The boat taken to sea with the storm surge, the house ruined beyond his means to repair it.

Sheryl, on the other hand, had struggled to find work after losing her job at the building department—something he felt was largely responsible for after recruiting her to help in stopping a crooked real estate deal. Together they had saved one of the pristine outer keys from development, but it had cost them. They had since been living together in his half-finished house to save money, but with the house in ruins and no income, they'd been forced to make the hard decision and move to Tampa. He'd had a reputation both as a fishing guide and a craftsman; someone who could handle the unusual, and wouldn't say no to a challenge. One of his regular bonefish clients had offered him a job rebuilding an old fish house on the intracoastal waterway near St. Petersburg. There had been little choice than to accept.

Before the storm, Sheryl had talked about getting out of the Keys, and maybe going back to school. She kept saying how the island life was no good for you. So this had seemed like the perfect answer - at least for her.

Moving to the real world was a little too close to reality for his hermit-like fishing guide lifestyle, and he was having a hard time adjusting. The construction job should be enough to get him back on his feet, though fishing was never far from his thoughts. He had done his homework and realized there was an opportunity in the rich waters of Tampa Bay and the Gulf of Mexico, but without the money to buy a boat, he needed another angle, and hoped paddle board fishing was going to be it. But first he needed her approval or at least acceptance of the idea.

"It's a little shaky. Do you think people can really do this?" she asked, as a wake from a distant boat passed underneath their boards.

He knew it was a major obstacle, but with the popularity of kayak fishing, this was sure to be the next big thing. The board, although not as stable as a kayak, offered the angler the freedom to move around and the vantage point of being above the water.

"These are stock boards," he said. "The ones I want to get are wider and more stable."

"Okay, so, Mr. Hot fishing guide, put me on a fish."

Will scanned the water for any indication that fish were feeding. A tail broke the surface of the five-foot-deep water and he pointed. "There. See it?"

She reeled her line in, adjusted her body, and cast a couple of feet in front of the tailing redfish, clicked the bail closed after the line sank, and started twitching the rod tip, reeling a little line each time. Suddenly the water exploded with a crash as the fish took the lure.

"Nice job! Now, hold the rod high and let it take some line. Maybe tighten the drag a hair."

The fish started its run, pulling line from the reel, and Sheryl gently turned the knob to increase the tension on the line. The fish slowed, tiring from the fight, and she began to pump the rod as she took back the line.

"Easy now, no herky jerky. He's going to make another run, just be ready and let him go," he said and watched the battle. It was almost as rewarding to coach an angler as it was to make the catch himself. "There, he turned his head. Get ready."

She held the rod high again, as he had taught her, letting it bend deeply to take the strain off the line. This run was shorter than the last, and soon the fish was visible. "I can see him!"

Will looked at her rod and saw the leader about to enter the rod tip. He went to his knees, pulled the line joining the boards to bring him closer, and leaned out for the fishing line, grabbed it and lifted the fish out of the water

The redfish glistened in the sun as he reached with his other hand, opened the cooler lid, and gently laid the flapping fish inside the box.

"Nice work." He went to high-five her, but she lost her balance, having to go onto her knees before she fell into the water.

Will untied the boards and lifted the anchor. They paddled the half-mile toward the Gandy Bridge, aiming for a small beach where they had launched. He landed first, pulled his board so the fin stuck in the sand, and went to help her.

One at a time he rolled the boards in the water to remove the sand and carried them to the gravel lot. With the boards loaded and gear stowed, they pulled two chairs from the back of the truck and carried them to the small beach where they sat down. There was something special about sunsets on Florida's west coast, he thought as they watched the sun start to blend with the horizon. He opened a bottle of wine and poured each of them a glass.

She was quiet—not a good sign. This was his last chance to sell her on a fishing gig. He was committed to the construction project, but knew that was a short term plan, not his future. He needed to get her agreement.

"Okay. I know you want to talk, so here's what I'm seeing. I love you, and don't want to cut you at the knees every time you come up with a plan, but--"

His heart sank, even though he'd been prepared for the denial. It was a risk, and one he would have taken had he been single. With enough money for a couple of boards and a used van, he would have no problem living the nomadic life for a while, but that wasn't for her. And his life had been so much richer since they met. He gazed at her crystal green eyes, which always reminded him of the clear water of the Keys.

"I know it's a stretch but--"

She took his hand. "I know it's your dream, and I'm not going to shut you down entirely. How about if you do it nights and weekends for a while, and see how it works?"

He nodded and sipped the wind. His spirit broken, he said, "I'm taking Lance from the fish house out tomorrow. He's been after me to look at that job of his. I'll finalize our deal." He put his head down, even though he had expected this outcome.

When she leaned over and kissed him, it felt more like a dog being patted on the head for obeying a command than a display of affection

* * *

The two men paddled the intracoastal waterway through Pass-A-Grille, a small community on the southern tip of the peninsula; just below more well known St Petersburg Beach. They had already caught and released a pair of barracuda that were on their way out to the Gulf to spawn. But they were in search of the more elusive snook, rumored to be in the waterway. Trolling may not be the best way to hook one, but Will had made the call due to the wind.

They'd put in five miles to the north and floated with the tide past several communities with large houses and docks on the water, interlaced with small restaurants and bars, on their downwind drift to the end of Pass-A-Grille beach. Under better circumstances, he would have stayed in this area, casting at the numerous docks and piles that provided cover for the fish, but the wind made that impossible. In fishing, one had to be versatile.

The versatile thing wasn't working so well in his personal life either, but he tried to put that out of his mind as the other man's rod bent over.

"Got one!" Will called over to him.

Lance went to his knees and removed the rod from the holder and set it in a pipe in the crate in front of him. He was an experienced angler, looking to board fishing as a challenge and a way to get into areas that were inaccessible by boat. He quickly had the fish next to the board and his free hand automatically moved to his side for the pliers sheathed on his belt. Reaching over the board, he grabbed the hook and shook the fish free.

"Another 'cuda." He sighed. "Can't grab a snook."

The loud music and roar of engines alerted Will that the boat was coming, just before its wake hit them. A moment later, a thirty-foot fishing boat settled into the water beside them. He looked the boat over, thinking it was an unusual mixture of form and function. Where one would expect a center console with a T-top, a small enclosed cabin sat in its place, large enough for two men to get out of the weather. The narrow beamed hull, powered by twin 275 HP engines, was a powerful mixture.

He thought it was probably just another obnoxious tourist, but Lance seemed to know him. They continued to paddle, with the boat keeping pace, until the music cut off and the man behind the wheel yelled over the sound of his engine.

"Yo, Baitman! You got a line on fixing that old building? Just say the word and I'll get it done for you. Season's almost here and that old cracker shack of yours looks like it's about to fall in the water," he yelled.

They were in an area where the intracoastal fanned out into a basin with houses on the Eastern side and marinas and restaurants on the West. Will followed Lance's gaze as he looked fondly at the old building. "No way. It needs to be done *right*, not your way."

"You never know. One storm and it could be gone. Tomorrow, next week, who knows. And, the big boys are starting to run out there!" the man yelled. He punched the throttle and drove off.

Just as they regained their balance from the initial wake, it was redirected by the seawall back toward them.

"Can we stop here for a minute? There's an empty slip." Lance went to his knees and pointed toward a small marina.

"Sure." Will guided his board to the empty dock, set his butt on the warm wood, and swung his feet onto the dock. He quickly looped the board's leash around a cleat, securing it, and went to help Lance.

They sat side by side on the dock drinking a beer from the cooler. "You want to tell me what that was about?" Will asked.

"That building," The man pointed to a decrepit fish house almost entirely built out over the water. "It's a unique spot. They won't let you build structures out over the water like that anymore. That's the job I called you for."

Will had wondered when he was going to get around to this. Sure, Lance was an avid fisherman, but he was also a businessman. Will felt set up, but was immediately curious. He evaluated the building with a carpenter's eye, wishing he didn't have eyeballs calibrated from years of experience as he surveyed it. Nothing was plumb or square, and the building dipped toward the water. The old metal siding was hanging on by the remains of long rusted nails, and the old galvanized metal roof was badly rusted. The interior was open to the elements, the windows long removed. The wind moved a piece of siding and a handful of pigeons flew from one of the broken windows.

"Doesn't look too good."

"I want you to have an open mind here." Lance drank a long sip of his beer and paused. "I know you need some work, and I think this building is your answer. There's no one else I know that has your skill-set."

Will thought he had reached the bottom just having to consider a real job, but looking at the building, he realized he'd misjudged how far he could fall. "That thing needs to be torn down."

"I'd be right there with you ... but I can't. That building has been in my family for several generations. Look around; there's nothing built over the water like that anymore. The Army Corp of Engineers and the city planners won't let it happen. And there's not enough land for a building and parking." He paused. "I'm looking to move the fish business over here. We're by the railroad tracks now; used to work back in the day when everything went by train, but these days it's all air freight. The neighborhood's rundown and after the bubble burst a few years ago, the building's not worth half what I refinanced it for."

Will looked at him skeptically. "Rebuild it? That thing looks like a good blow would take it into the water."

"It's been through a few of those," he laughed. "But I had an engineer look at it, and he thinks it's doable. I just need the right person. Someone open minded and creative." He patted Will on the back.

Will looked at the building again with fresh eyes, now that it was all out in the open. It would be a challenge, and if he had to get a job, he might as well be his own boss. Besides, working on the water, across from Pass-A-Grille Beach and on the intracoastal, wasn't a bad location.

The man must have seen his interest. "It's yours. No bids, no budgets. Just keep it moving. I'll give you free rein to do the work as you see fit."

Will looked at the man. This kind of offer from almost anyone else would have pegged his bullshit meter into the red, but he'd known Lance for years. If a man's character was represented in the way he fished, Lance was to be trusted.

"Sounds good. What about plans and permits?" He hesitated, hating to talk money. "And you know I'm pretty broke right now. I can't finance this and bill you. I need the money up front."

"Will." He looked at him. "You make this work, I'll pay you cash. As far as permits, I'll leave that up to you, but you've got to know that people are going to be watching this job, and not all of them are going to like it. There's a bunch of people here that don't want this to go forward; some want it torn down, and others are looking to buy it for themselves. So you're going to have to watch your back."

Chapter 2

Will opened the padlock on the makeshift door. The slab of plywood, reinforced with two-by-fours, opened slowly, the rusty gate hinges squealing in resistance. They entered and started to look around, Sheryl staying close as they picked their way around the piles of debris scattered around the floor.

Light streamed through the openings where windows had once hung and penetrated the gaps in the siding and roof.

"Will. This is a really big job!"

"Yeah, it's a challenge, though."

"You know how to do all this stuff? I mean your house in the Keys…" She paused. "It was really beautiful, all the finish work you did, and the design was really cool."

He didn't want to think about what he had lost, so he refocused on the present. "I built some docks and stuff when I was just out of high school. It's the same principle, just on a bigger scale. The biggest problem is getting some help."

"There are some kids at the club that would probably work during the day for you."

She had started working as a waitress several nights a week while taking classes during the day. Will was skeptical about hiring bar workers, knowing their penchant for late-night parties and sleeping all day. But he stayed quiet, not wanting to upset the tranquility with an argument. And he didn't have anyone else.

"I know an engineer that can help me get this going with the city. Guess I should start there."

"I'm so proud of you." She leaned over and kissed him.

He smiled, but was torn inside; he was pandering to her, badly wanting her respect, and knew that he'd do anything to get it.

Finally, having seen enough, he led her toward the door and outside. The building locked, they got into the old truck and were about to pull out of the lot when a black pickup pulled in. Music vibrated through the tinted windows and Will looked with disgust toward the hidden driver. Guys that drove trucks like that were invariably the same guys that owned speed boats. His theory was confirmed when the window slid down, revealing the same guy that had been behind the wheel of the boat in the intracoastal.

A quick look and a head nod, meant to be intimidating, and the truck screeched out of the parking lot. Will wondered if this is what Lance meant when he said to watch his back.

* * *

Will sat at the drafting table, waiting for Emerson to review his sketch. The old man had been old years ago, when Will met him working on one of his projects in the Keys. Surprised he was still working, he was relieved when he had answered the phone and agreed to meet. The office, once full of draftsmen, was now deserted—just a middle-aged Cuban lady working at an adjacent table.

"Well, you think it'll work?" Will asked after several minutes of silence.

Emerson didn't appear to hear what he said, but continued to look at the drawing. Finally he looked up and took off his glasses. "I'd like to look firsthand, but from what you have here, it's not a problem. The building is lightweight; little more than a dock with a roof. We need to beef up the substructure, so that's going to be a challenge, working on it from the water, but this kind of thing is right up your alley."

Will breathed in relief that the old man was onboard. Finding an engineer was the first and probably biggest hurdle he would face. If Emerson had declined, the project was dead. Younger engineers were over cautious, and would insist on tearing down the structure. Rebuilding the piers and beams wouldn't be easy, with the structure overhead, but it *could* be done. He had spent a sleepless night figuring out different approaches to accomplish it, and then brought the plans with his ideas to Emerson.

"I need help with the permit too," he said, hoping the comment would slide by without resistance. Emerson had a contractor's license so old that it was back in the single digits. Will hoped he would sign the permit papers as the contractor of record.

"Well," Emerson started, "we've done it before, don't suppose it'll hurt."

Will smiled. "Want to take a ride and check it out?"

"Well, now you're talking, young man."

* * *

Will sat on the seawall next to the building and checked his dive gear. He had spent the morning measuring and sketching the existing structure, using his paddleboard to float underneath to check the beam sizes and spacing. Now he needed to have a look underwater and check the condition of the piers that supported the structure.

He spit in his mask and rinsed it from a bottle of water sitting next to him, put the fins on over his booties, and lowered the mask onto his face. Carefully, he kneeled onto the board floating next to him, and used his hands to paddle out to deeper water. He wasn't sure what the bottom looked like or how dangerous it was, so he moved the board to one of the piers, furthest from land at the end of the building, and tied the leash around it. Confident the water was at least six feet here, he slid off the board and looked around the murky water. The tide had clouded up the water and he finned back to the board and grabbed the dive light.

The beam cut through the silt, showing the first pier. He raised his head out of the water and took a large breath, then dove to check the pier's base. The wooden pole was old, and covered with barnacles below the water line, making it impossible to see any decay without chiseling the mollusks off the wood. That would be difficult to do without tanks or solid footing, so he moved on.

He encountered the same conditions at the next line of piers, placed several feet closer to the seawall. At the next row, the water became shallow and he was able to kneel in the sand and place his face in the water. Able to work without the strain of constantly surfacing for air, he took the dive knife strapped to his calf and began the tedious process of chipping the mollusks off the old wood.

Slowly, the old, treated wood revealed itself. Scar marks from the knife showed clean, unblemished wood, and he was able to poke the knife directly into the pier now. With a picture of the main floor of the building in his head, he realized that this was one of the areas the floor sagged. His suspicions proved accurate as the knife slid easily into the wood, indicating that it was rotten. The building was sagging because its support structure was failing.

His survey complete, he was about to climb out of the water, when something caught his eye. The shine of chrome in the parking lot was visible reflected like a spotlight into the foot-high gap between the floor structure and seawall. Mask pulled back on his head, he took off his fins and stood hunched in the small space.

Two massive legs stared back at him.

"What do we have here, Jacque Freakin' Cousteau? Nobody in their right mind dives in that shit. You looking for old Jose Gaspar's lost treasure, or what?"

Will thought about sliding back into the water to avoid a confrontation, but his choice was made for him when he glanced up and saw two beady black eyes staring at him.

"Come on out of there. I think me and you need to have a talk," the guy with the eyes said.

Reluctantly, Will crawled out from below the building, his only relief being that he could now stand erect. "Something I can help you with?" He looked past the man at the truck; it was the same black truck that had cruised through the lot the day before. He couldn't help but notice the blond hair blowing in the air conditioning from the passenger seat, almost translucent in the sun.

"Me and you gotta reach an agreement here. You're the same guy that was over here with the old man the other day. What's he got up his sleeve?" The guy paused, and looked toward the girl in the truck.

She caught his look and whined, "Can we go now? I'm hungry."

"Shut up, bitch. I've got business here." He turned back to Will, who couldn't avoid staring at the girl. "You want a piece of that? Just cooperate. Show him some boob," he yelled at the truck. The girl rose up in the seat, stuck her tongue out and pulled aside her blouse."

Will just stared.

"Now back to business. Old Lance has his timetable and I have mine. You see, I can get a little impatient about slow work." He winked.

Will was about to nod his head in acceptance when he glanced at the girl and noticed the piercing blue eyes staring at him.

"Gregori, I thought you were the mayor," the girl interrupted.

"I already told you to shut up. I'm all the mayor you need." He looked back at Will, his face and neck red.

Before Will could respond, he turned and walked toward the driver's side door of the truck and hopped in. The tail pipes roared as he accelerated out of the parking lot, horns blaring as he cut off several cars.

Will stood there in his booties and board shorts, not sure what to make of the man, then gathered his gear and placed it in the large metal toolbox he had set inside the building. Surely the guy was just blowing smoke, hoping to scare him. He'd worked for impatient customers before, but this kind of job wasn't something you could rush. He checked his watch, changed, and locked up. He would have to hurry to make his appointment with Emerson at the building department.

Chapter 3

Will sat at the bar nursing his beer and watching Sheryl as she worked the crowd. She cast a wary look his way when she passed by. Several weeks ago there had been an incident where he had a few too many beers and almost gotten her fired. Since then, she had forbidden him from hanging out. This time, she had given him a pass in order to meet Kyle and Dick. But she was clearly keeping an eye on him. He had been there for an hour now, waiting for her shift to end.

Avoiding her glance, he looked out the big plate glass window at the street. The old cigar center of Tampa, Ybor City, now converted to a nightlife hub, was just starting to get busy. The old brick buildings had been renovated into bars and restaurants, and the area had proven to be a hotspot.

Will admired the feel of the place. The brick walls had been left intact, as well as the original ceiling framing. The bar was the old cigar counter, scarred with burns acquired over a hundred years of fallen ash. His only problem as he watched the boisterous crowd work their way past the bouncer was that Sheryl had to work here. She had years of experience with government, but claimed she was fed up and burnt out on the bureaucracy—especially after being fired from the building department in Marathon. She was going to the University of South Florida part time, looking forward to a career in environmental studies. It wasn't like she was sitting on the couch eating bonbons, either. Truth was, she brought in more money than he did.

Tired from working on the fish house by himself all day, he had taken her up on her offer to find help. The two bar backs were due in any time now, and she'd told him that they were looking to supplement their current Friday and Saturday nights' income. He was hesitant to hire anyone, though. Besides not having workers' compensation insurance, something he couldn't get without a license, he was used to working alone. Not one to give orders or teach, he preferred the solitude of the craftsman.

But as he arched his back to ease the building stiffness from the day's work, he knew he needed young blood to supplement his skills. If he didn't get help, he wouldn't be able to finish the job. And he needed the money.

Lost in thought, he looked up to see two kids standing in front of him. "Can I help you guys?"

"Hey, you Will, man?" the taller asked.

Will chuckled to himself as he sized up the pair. They looked young. Really young. The taller boy had the gawky look of a teenager who hadn't grown into his body yet. The smaller—who was only smaller in height, as he was as wide as he was tall, with the build of a linebacker and a nose that had obviously been broken at least once—stared at him with an odd look on his face.

Will looked at both boys' bloodshot eyes and confirmed his suspicion—typical bar workers, they were stoned.

"Yeah." He sipped his beer.

"Sheryl your old lady?" the taller one continued.

"You're full of questions. What can I do for you?"

"I'm Kyle, and this here's Dick," the taller one said. "If you're the right dude, she said you were looking for some help. Some kind of construction thing."

Sipping his beer, he felt old as he looked at them. He was

sure they were too young, but figured if they worked at the bar, they had to be at least twenty-one. They looked strong enough, although he wasn't sure they could get out of bed in the morning.

"I'm not sure this is right for you guys."

Dick moved his heavy frame toward him. "We can do whatever it is you want. We pretty much shovel shit and clean up puke around here. Don't think we can't handle what you have."

Will thought for a minute, and realized he'd better take what he was given. "Can you boys show up before noon? I need people that can get to work early."

They looked at each other, but before they could respond, Sheryl walked up behind them. "Of course they can. Just give them a chance. They work hard here."

Will could see that the odds were stacked against him now, with Sheryl on the case. "I know it's Friday night and you have to work late, but I want to work this weekend and get a head start." His goal was to get at least one new pile set before Monday, to make sure his idea would work without the prying eyes of the building inspector on him. He suspected that in a small beach town word would get out fast about the project. There wasn't much other construction going on and he was guessing the building inspector would be a constant visitor — invited or not.

He caught the quick glance the two boys exchanged during his silence.

"Yeah, we're in. But can we start early?"

Surprised, he gave them directions to the job and asked them to be there at seven am.

Sheryl kissed his cheek. "Thanks. They won't let you down. I'm out of here, you ready?"

Will didn't have to be asked twice. He fished in his pocket, left a twenty on the bar, downed what remained of his beer, and was halfway out the door before she caught up to him.

* * *

Greg cut the lights as he coasted to a stop at the fish house, leaving the black truck almost invisible in the dark parking lot. He left the engine running to power the air conditioning, keeping the cab cool as he waited. The truck was pulled into a space between a small square structure adjacent to the main building and the Pass-A-Grille Marina next door. Twilight had just finished its nightly stint, and it was dark now as he watched the waterway. Boats passed by slowly, moving through the no-wake zone, their presence identified only by their running lights. Most were small pleasure boats, returning from a day on the water. He reached into a cooler behind the seat and pulled out a beer, ready to settle in and wait.

An hour passed and he started getting fidgety, the cool air conditioning the only thing keeping him calm. Getting more anxious as the minutes clicked by on the dashboard clock, he felt the wad of cash in his pocket and started running worst case scenarios through his head. If the fishing boat making the delivery was stopped and boarded, he might lose some profits, but he knew he had nothing to fear, these guys were loyal to him and wouldn't talk. Normally he would have made the trip himself, but he'd just gotten back yesterday with the first bluefin of the season. It looked to be a promising year so he'd decided to recruit some fresh blood to supplement his income. There was always the chance that Fish and Game would try and run a sting operation, but he only dealt with people he knew—mostly childhood friends. In past years, it had been just him and a couple of buddies running the operation, but with the price for the prize tuna at an all time high, he had started to branch out.

Finally a boat stopped and flashed a spotlight three times at the shore—the signal they were ready to dock. He removed a flashlight from the console next to him and checked the parking lot. Satisfied they weren't being watched, he flashed the light three times at the boat, then reluctantly turned off the ignition and left the comfort of the truck. He walked to the seawall, where he waited as the boat backed slowly into the tight space.

Two men jumped off, both with lines in their hands, and looped them around two nearby pilings. A third man came from behind the wheel and tossed one of the men a line tied to a cleat at midship and then jumped onto the dock. The man scrambled forward on the decaying wood and looped it around a pile in front of the boat, to keep the boat from drifting backward.

"Good. You still remember to take precautions," Greg said to the man as he watched the crew work. The men were holding the dock lines now, with just a single turn on the cleats for leverage and a quick getaway.

"Always. Now let's get this done." He glanced nervously over his shoulder at the boat traffic. "I don't like doing this on the weekend. Too much traffic."

"It'll be worth your while." Greg knew the timing was undesirable, but he had no choice. Originally, the delivery had been scheduled for Sunday night, when boat traffic would be much lighter; but a storm moving into the Gulf had accelerated the schedule.

"What do you have?"

"Four jewfish, about a hundred pounds each, plus two coolers of snapper and grouper. Got a small marlin, too." He signaled for the two crewmen to start unloading the catch. "Had a bluefin on, too. Must have gone four hundred, but we lost it. First one this year."

"Good. Let's have a look." Greg reached into the pocket of his cargo shorts and removed a key chain. Selecting a key, he opened the padlock on the door of the square building next to them. Cold air blasted from the cooler. He turned on the light and waited for the crewmen to bring the catch in.

"What the hell? This is all supposed to be gutted and skinned!"

"Got most of it, but it was too bumpy to finish. Can't afford to have one of the guys lose a finger out there."

"Shit." Greg stood to the side and watched as the men unloaded the contents of three coolers onto a tarp placed on the stainless steel floor. They went back to the boat and returned with another tarp carried awkwardly between them. Once they were inside, they unrolled it to reveal a two-hundred-pound marlin.

Greg reached into his pocket and removed the cash he had been fondling. He peeled off twelve hundreds and paid the man, who grabbed the money and signaled his men toward the boat. Greg followed behind them, turning off the light and locking the door. He took a quick look at the street before climbing back into his truck and pulling out of the lot.

He drove back toward US19 and turned left, driving automatically as he calculated the profits in his head. He was discouraged that they had lost the bluefin, but he'd lost his share of the behemoth tuna as well. Catching them on rod and reel from a small boat was far from a sure thing. The fish they brought in would net him a five-thousand-dollar profit, and there would be plenty of bluefin as they moved into the Gulf to spawn. It was good news that the bluefin were starting to run. That was what he waited for every year. A good quality fish could bring in ten to twenty grand.

A smile crossed his face as he pulled up to the valet stand in the crowded parking lot of the strip. Before he got out, he reached into the glove compartment and removed a gold Rolex watch. He put the watch on his wrist and admired it.

The valet greeted him by name and Greg tossed him the keys as he climbed down onto the running board and stepped onto the sidewalk.

* * *

"Thanks for giving those guys some work. They've been complaining about only having the weekend nights at the club, and not having enough rent money."

"Let's hope it works. I could use some help. Tomorrow will tell if they can actually show up and work."

Will leaned back against the headrest and watched the throngs of partiers packing the sidewalk. He jerked forward as Sheryl dodged a group jay-walking with no regard for traffic. There had been no discussion about her driving after the beers he had. Leaning back again, he thought about how there had been no discussion about a *lot* of things, lately. His life in the Keys had been simpler, almost removed from reality. But that was gone with the hurricane, and he knew she was good for him — at least he hoped she was. It was his own lack of planning and insurance that had him in this spot.

Now, she planned for both of them, and though that was probably for the best, at least financially, he felt imprisoned.

"They'll be there. Bet they stay up all night."

He hadn't thought about that, but she was right. They wouldn't get out of work until four am. Maybe that was what the glance he'd caught was about. The next morning would tell if they can hack it or not.

"The owner asked me to work tomorrow night," she said suddenly.

Earlier in the week, they had fought over her working weekend nights. He hated the idea of her in that kind of environment. The money was good, but now that he had work, he figured she could just take shifts during the week, go to school, and be happy. It really wouldn't upset him if she quit altogether.

He stewed about the additional night as she pulled onto the Crosstown Expressway and followed the signs to the Gandy Bridge.

"I think that's a bad idea." He regretted it the minute the words were out of his mouth

"You do. Well, I haven't seen a paycheck come out of your pocket in awhile."

He stared out of the window, watching the anchor lights of the boats fishing under the bridge bounce in the chop. They crossed the bay in silence. He had to figure out how to make this right with her. Their only problem was money, and that was his fault.

Desperate, he touched her hand. She didn't withdraw it, but she didn't respond, either.

Chapter 4

Will drove to the jobsite the next morning wondering if his help was going to be there and if they were, what kind of condition they would be in. He parked and went toward the old Ford Fiesta, noticing the Grateful Dead decal on the window of the faded blue car and two heads slumped against their windows. Kyle jumped when he tapped the glass with his key.

"Morning. Glad you guys made it."

"Huh?" He rolled down the window. "Oh, sure thing man," he muttered as he smacked Dick on the shoulder. The other boy woke with a start, striking back automatically.

"Take your time. I have to get some things organized." Will walked away, distinctly aware of the smell of pot that came from the car when the window was rolled down. He hoped it was out of their systems now. Not a smoker himself, he had a feeling the boys had started to supply Sheryl. She hadn't smoked in Marathon, at least not in front of him, but since she'd started working at the club, it had become a nightly indulgence.

He didn't say much, as these days she was more pleasant on it than off it.

The padlock popped open, and he yanked on the temporary plywood door leading to the interior of the building. It was surprisingly cool inside; the water below the structure having a cooling effect at night. That would soon wear off, though, as he heard the first creak of the corrugated metal roof. Once the sun was out and the roof heated up, the building would be a sauna.

He went back to his truck to get the concrete saw he had rented. Cutting the concrete floor above where the new posts would be installed was the first step in his plan. With any luck, he could do the layout and show the boys how to operate the saw. He then planned on picking up a couple of poles while they cut the square holes and removed the concrete from the floor.

Kyle and Dick rounded the corner as he was bringing the saw in.

"Hey, can one of you get the hose and gas can from my truck?"

Dick went for the truck, while Kyle followed him into the building.

"I'm going below to drill some pilot holes up through the floor. Can you keep an eye out for them and mark them with this?" He handed him a can of spray paint.

It took a half-hour of work below the building to move the paddle board around the piers to the locations where he wanted the new poles to be installed and drill small holes up through the deck. On his knees, he paddled with his hands back to the seawall and climbed off the board, securing it to a cleat.

Back in the building, he saw the boys sitting against a wall, clearly looking tired.

"Come on." He looked around at the dots of paint on the floor where he had drilled his holes; at least so far they had followed directions. He went for his tool bag. With their help, he measured off each hole, using the marks as centers and drawing a three-foot square around each one.

"I'm going to do the first one with you, and then go for materials while you do the others."

He reached into a paper bag and handed them ear and eye

protection; the boys looked at him like he was crazy, but followed his lead as he put them on. Ready, he grabbed the saw from the ground.

"Hook that hose up and turn the nozzle to a small stream of water. One of you needs to hold it in front of the blade to keep the dust down."

With the choke opened and fuel primed, he pulled the start cord of the saw and waited for it to warm up. Once the motor evened out, he nodded toward Kyle, who held the hose.

The boy immediately opened the nozzle, flooding the floor.

Will gave a signal to lower the flow, then, with water gently streaming onto the concrete, lowered the blade to the floor and squeezed the trigger. The saw increased rpms and he slowly put it down on the painted line.

Sparks flew and the noise became deafening as the blade bit into the concrete. Kyle increased the water flow slightly to keep down the dust as the saw's diamond blade started to make its way along the line. Will jerked when the blade sparked, and the saw kicked back when it hit the steel reinforcement half way through the 4-inch-thick material.

With his core tightened and the saw revved higher this time, Will set the blade back in the hole and finished the cut.

"You guys do the next one. Slow and steady." He wanted to make sure they had a handle on this before he left. Dick went for the saw, leaving Kyle holding the hose. He revved the engine and jammed the blade into the concrete, almost falling backward when it kicked back.

Will placed a hand on his shoulder and made a downward motion with his hands, telling him to slow down.

The boy tried again, a determined look on his face. The saw cooperated this time, and the cut went smoothly.

"Okay. When you've cut all four sides, you can try and pry the piece out with this." He handed them a long steel bar with a flat end. "If it won't go, cut two diagonal lines and make the pieces smaller. You may have to cut the wire inside the concrete with these." He showed them a large set of bolt cutters.

"Won't it just fall through?" Kyle asked.

"No. There's plywood underneath it. We'll cut that later, with a different saw."

The building was heating up, and sweat poured off Dick as he revved the saw for another cut. Will went to his thermos and poured a cup of coffee, watching the boys as he drank. Satisfied they had it under control, he finished the cup, screwed it back on the thermos, and left. It would take him an hour or two to pick up the poles, and hopefully the boys would be done when he returned.

* * *

They were through the third hole when Dick turned the saw off. "I need some air."

"Sure, man," Kyle said as he turned the hose off.

They walked out of the building, seeking shade, but the sun was high overhead now. "It's freakin' hot. If you would have fixed the AC in the car, we could chill in there."

"Will didn't say anything about breaks," Kyle said, ignoring the comment.

"Dude." Dick looked at Kyle. "Screw that. I need to cool off. You got any of that weed left?"

"A little." Kyle headed to the car.

Dick looked around the parking lot baking in the late morning heat. The angle of the sun was above the building's roof, and there was no shade to be found. He walked toward the three-story-high steel building the Pass-A-Grille Marina used to store their dry dock boats, and noticed the small, square cooler adjacent to the fish house. Curious, he walked over to the door and jiggled the lock. The compressor kicked on just as he touched it, startling him, but he realized what it was and had an idea.

"Hey, man, bring those bolt cutters over here," he yelled to Kyle. There was no reason he could think of *not* to enjoy the cool air inside.

Kyle came back with the cutters. "What the fuck, man? You can't just cut somebody's lock off."

"Do you see anyone around? Why is this thing even running? The place is closed." He took the cutters from Kyle and opened the jaws, placing the steel shackle inside. The cutters closed around the lock and met resistance. With another push, the metal parted and the jaws met. "Now let's chill. You got the weed?" He twisted the broken lock until it separated and he could manipulate it out of the hasp. The door opened, and he was given a taste of the cool air inside.

"This is gonna be classic. Our own chill box." He stepped in, leaving the door open for Kyle. "Turn on the light. I can't see anything," he said as he took a pipe from his pocket.

Kyle ran his hands against the door jamb, found a switch, and turned the light on.

Dick was the first to jump. "Holy shit man. It's a freakin' marlin. Look at that son of a bitch." He went toward the fish and ran his hand down the bill.

"Dick, something's wrong here." Kyle was looking at the bags and carcasses of the other fish. "This is all illegal. The fishing season for snapper and grouper is closed, and no one keeps billfish."

The boys were both avid fishermen; though restricted to the smaller bay because of money, they knew the law. Both knew Fish and Game were constantly parked at the boat ramps, looking for illegal catches.

"Well, whatever. It's cool in here." Dick stuffed the bowl of the pipe and pulled a lighter from his pocket. The flame flickered, and he had to shield it from the cool air blowing from the evaporator coil. Finally the bowl caught, and he inhaled deeply, holding his breath as he handed the pipe to Kyle.

A horn blared, causing Kyle to drop the pipe. He picked it up and they slid outside, closing the door behind them. A white sedan with the insignia of the city sat in front of the fish house. He relaxed when he saw it wasn't the police and watched as a man got out of the car, wearing shorts and a polo shirt walk towards the plywood door of the building.

"We gotta see what he wants," Kyle said.

"Yeah, you go." Dick slunk away toward their car.

Kyle expected the reaction, knowing Dick's disdain for authority. He went toward the door and walked into the building. The man was looking at one of the holes they'd cut.

"Hey. Can I help you?" Kyle asked.

"Building inspector." He showed Kyle the credential hanging from a lanyard around his neck. "You doing this work?"

"Yes, sir. Working for the contractor. He should be back anytime."

"Listen, I know he got a permit for the job, but we have some rules you need to follow here." He reached into his back pocket, removed several pieces of paper, and handed them to Kyle. "Noise is a big deal, and we got several calls about you guys this morning. You can't be doing this on weekends—only during the week. The hours are all on the paper there."

"Okay, I'll pass it on. We're pretty tired, anyway."

"I'll give you a verbal warning this time. Just make sure it doesn't happen again." He turned to leave. "And one more thing." He handed him a business card. "I need to speak to the contractor. Whatever you guys are up to, it's not on the plan."

* * *

Will pulled back into the lot and was surprised the site was quiet. He figured the guys would still be working on the holes.

Backing the truck toward the door, he left the tip of the poles as close as he could get them to the entrance. He got out and went inside. The building was deserted, and he saw two holes still left to cut.

He looked at his watch, it was only one and they should still be working. Outside the building, he looked around and saw the two heads slumped forward in the car.

"Hey! I knew you guys couldn't pull this off," he screamed at them.

Kyle stirred from the driver's seat and looked toward him. "Building inspector came by and said we couldn't make noise on Saturday." He handed Will the papers and the business card through the open window. "Wants to talk to you, too."

"Shit." Will scanned the papers in amazement. There were more rules here than a Catholic school for wayward girls. How was he ever going to get anything done?

"You guys can clean up and put away the tools. I guess we're shut down for the day." He looked at his truck. "Have to get those poles inside before you go, though."

"No problem. We can be back Monday." Kyle smacked Dick to wake him, dodging the reflexive strike back.

Dick rubbed his eyes. "Dude. You need to check out that cooler over there."

"What for?" Will asked.

"Your old lady said you were a fishing guide in the Keys. You need to see this." Dick got out of the car and walked toward the cooler.

Will followed reluctantly, wondering how the boys had found time to get in trouble when they should have been working. Finally they came to a stop in front of the door, and he saw that the lock had been cut. Before he could say, anything Dick opened the door and he was assaulted by the smell of pot.

He glared at Dick. "What the—"

Dick cut him off before he could say anything. "Just look, okay?"

Will turned on the switch and stepped inside, trying not to breathe too deeply. What he saw shocked him. A marlin carcass and several huge bags of fish. He walked by the marlin and picked up a bag of meat. "Snapper. Looks like American Red, and this is jewfish."

"Exactly," Dick said.

"You guys go clean up the job. We'll talk about this later." Will stared at the fish on the floor wondering how this was going to affect the job. He suspected that this might have something to do with the conflict between Lance and Greg as well as the big man's threats. Turning away he shut off the light and closed the door. He needed to focus on what mattered right now — and that was getting a paycheck. Will wanted to get the place cleaned up before Lance arrived. He would deal with the broken lock, pot smoking, and fish later.

They quickly had the job organized and the poles unloaded quickly. Will stood in the doorway and watched the boys pull out. It hadn't been the day he had planned, but it might be enough work to get the payment he had asked for.

Chapter 5

Will sat on a curb in the only shaded spot in the lot and thumbed the inspector's card. The pages of regulations lay at his feet, quickly spreading out in the light breeze. He had been taught carpentry at an early age, and clearly had talent as a craftsman, but the rigors of being a contractor differed vastly from those of a craftsman. Always trying to build something faster and cheaper, customers and general contractors had forced him out of the trade years ago.

He'd thought he could get back into it. But the visit by the inspector and the regulations at his feet had dampened his spirit for the project.

The fish in the cooler were also on his mind. It should have been none of his business, but he couldn't help but wonder what was going on. The cooler full of what he was sure were illegally caught fish—especially the marlin—offended his sense of right. He didn't always agree with the regulations passed by the bureaucrats in Tallahassee, but he followed them, nevertheless. He had worked for years as a guide, making his living primarily from catch and release. Witnessing the decline of the fisheries firsthand, he feared if they didn't recover from the abuse of overfishing and poaching, fishing for many species would be shut down entirely, ruining it for everyone. To further complicate things, if he called in the authorities and revealed what they had found, the job was likely to be shut down as a crime scene.

"Will."

He looked up and noticed Lance's car.

"You all right?"

"Yeah. Just thinking about some stuff." He got up and went toward the building, meeting Lance at the door.

"You guys started already. That's great."

"The city is not so hot on it. The inspector came by earlier and shut us down. Some kind of noise thing on the weekends."

"I should have warned you about that," Lance said. "They can be real ball-busters here. Let's see what you got done."

Will guided him through the building, explaining the work they had done and what he intended to do next.

Lance wiped his brow. "Let's go talk outside."

Will walked behind him as they left the building. The sun had receded enough to allow some of the taller trees to cast their shadows over sections of the lot now and they stood in the shade. He waited for Lance to talk.

"I was hoping to see some more work," Lance started.

Will's heart sank. He desperately needed the draw that Lance had promised.

"But, I understand the city stuff. Nothing you can do about that." He reached into his pocket and took out an envelope. "Here's five grand, which should cover your expenses, but I'm going to need to see some serious progress early next week, before I can give you any more."

Will took the envelope and put it in his back pocket. "Thanks."

Lance started to walk away, but Will stopped him.

"Can I ask you something? You're in the fish business."

"Sure."

"In fact, maybe you should just look at it and let me know

what you think." He led the way to the cooler and reached for the door. "One of my guys found this."

"I rent that out to a local guy. We shouldn't be going in there," Lance said.

"Like I said, one of my guys stumbled in here. Found something I think you should probably see." He opened the door, turned on the light, and stood aside to let Lance past.

Will stayed outside, allowing Lance the time and space he needed to make his own conclusions. A minute later, the other man emerged.

"Well, the circumstances of finding this aside, I'm glad you showed it to me," Lance said.

"So?" Will asked, relieved.

"You know what it is as well as I do. But what to do about it?"

"That's why I showed it to you. I thought about calling Fish and Game, but it's your property. I didn't want to step on your toes."

"I appreciate that. It's one of the reasons that I have you working on the building—you've got good sense, especially when it comes to keeping your mouth shut. With my business, this could look really bad, being on my property and all." He shut the door. "I've got some contacts I can call Monday."

"Cool. I'll wait to hear from you then."

"By the way, you might warn your guys to stay away from this. The guy I rent it to has a mean streak."

Will walked Lance to his car and shook his hand again. He was grateful for his understanding in Dick's trespass, and he *did* seem concerned about the fish.

He walked over to the building and locked the door. The boats docked at the marina next door caught his eye as he went to his truck. Sheryl was working tonight, so he had no reason to rush home.

He walked by the three-story steel building and peered inside at the boats sitting four high on steel racks, then headed to the dock, where some of the sailboats were tied up at a series of piers. One boat caught his eye; a For Sale sign taped to its cabin window. He went toward the boat, looked around, and hopped on. The sailboat looked to be about twenty-eight feet with a tiller. The companionway was locked, but he walked around the deck and looked inside the small windows. There was a small kitchen and a v-berth in the bow. Back in the cockpit, he sat down on one of the benches and stared out at the water.

The fish in the walk-in cooler and Lance's reaction were still bothering him. Although he'd seemed concerned, Lance had not been as proactive as Will would have liked. By Monday the fish could be gone.

He thought again about taking matters into his own hands, but was conflicted; poaching violated his moral compass to the point that he almost didn't care about violating Lance's trust. In the end, it came down to money.

The best compromise he could make with himself was to try and gain some information to pass on. If he hung around and kept an eye on things, he could see who picked up the fish and have that information to give to Lance, they could set up a sting and catch the guy off the property. That would keep the heat off the building project and stop the poaching.

He looked back toward the fish house and cooler, realizing he had the perfect vantage point to observe any activity from the boat. It was comfortable sitting here, since the marina building was now blocking the setting sun, placing the deck in the shade. Will relaxed and couldn't help but close his eyes.

* * *

Headlights flashed across his face, waking him from a sound sleep and it took a few seconds for him to realize where he was and what he was doing. From the height of the moon in the sky, the sun had been down for a while. The lights turned away as the truck parked and illuminated the cooler now.

Will got up slowly and stayed low as he moved off the boat and onto the dock. He crept toward the seawall, doing his best to stay in the shadows. A curse called out in a strange language startled him, and he figured the missing lock had been discovered. The light went on and the silhouette of a large man moved inside.

Will didn't dare get closer, but crouched down in the darkness and watched. The man motioned toward the truck, and two figures emerged. They went to the cooler and started loading the fish into the bed of the truck. A few minutes later, the light went off and the door was shut. The two men were back in the truck, but instead of following, the larger man went toward the fish house door. He tried the lock and turned away, staring right at Will's truck.

"Fucking contractor," he muttered, heading back to his truck.

He waited, not sure what to do. There was no way he could follow them—the truck would be long gone before he could even get out of the parking lot. He leaned forward and tried to get a better look at the truck and maybe get the license plate. As it backed toward him, in a flash of recognition, he realized the man was the same guy that had threatened him the other day.

Back in the shadows, he waited for his heart to slow as the truck's tires screeched and it pulled onto the street. He cursed himself for leaving his truck here—now he was guilty by association. The confrontation and threats from the other day replayed in his head. Whoever that guy was, he meant trouble. And now he knew, or at least suspected, that Will had been in his cooler.

Shaken, he saw the neon sign down the street for a bar, and figured a beer wouldn't hurt. Maybe a local could tell him something about the guy in the truck.

He decided to walk the quarter-mile to the bar, figuring if the guy came back, he would think the truck was parked for the night and Will was gone. Five minutes later, he reached the bar and pulled the door open. It was Saturday night, and the place was pretty full; a typical beach bar, with an exposed rafter ceiling, unfinished concrete floors, and a bar front covered with corrugated metal.

He went to an empty spot at the bar and stood waiting for the bartender to come over. Suddenly two men came toward him.

"Hey, aren't you the guy working on the fish house?" one asked.

Will swallowed, not knowing if they were the men that had loaded the fish. "Yeah, that's me," he mumbled.

"Cool, man. I'm Doug and this is Marty. We saw that some work was being done there. Glad for it, too. We own a couple of stores down on the beach side, and having that building back in service would be great for the area. Any way we can help, let us know."

Will swallowed again, relieved. "Buy you guys a drink?" he asked.

"Sure."

The three men went to a table in the corner, and a waitress with the shortest shorts Will had ever seen came over to take their order. A few minutes later, she was back with three beers. They clinked bottles and drank, the men asking Will about his background, fascinated with his stories about the Keys.

Several beers later, Will got the courage to ask about the man. "You guys know a big guy, drives a lifted black truck?"

They exchanged glances. "That's Greg Borkowski. Not one of our better residents. He give you trouble?" Doug asked.

Will told them of the exchange and threats from the other day, leaving the details of the fish out.

"Yeah, he's a bad dude. Thinks he can bully everyone around and get things his way. Lots of rumors about him, too, although no one's ever proven any. Best to steer clear of that one," Marty said.

Will sighed, wondering if he would have a choice.

* * *

Ybor City on a Saturday night looked more like Times Square than an old cigar town. The area had been built in a different era, not designed for the massive traffic caused by the influx of bars. Will navigated carefully, trying to find a parking space. Normally he would have taken pains to find a free spot, but with a half-dozen beers in his system, he was over both his own limit and the law's, making him anxious to get off the road.

Finally, a spot opened and he backed in. Car horns blared as he missed the mark on the first few attempts, all but stopping traffic on the narrow street. He opened the door; realizing he was still two feet away from the curb, but not caring he stepped out and locked the truck. The crowds became thicker as he made his way toward Fourth Street and the club. Groups of twenty-somethings were out in force, spilling off the sidewalks and forcing foot traffic onto the street. He slid sideways around people and parked cars as he made his way toward the bar.

There was a short line at the door, but a quick word with the bouncer and Will was allowed in. The action on the street was nothing compared to the bar. Music assaulted him as he eased between the mass of people, trying to make a path to the waitress station on the far side of the bar. He spotted Sheryl as she worked the crowd like a running back, a tray full of drinks hoisted above her head, her free hand extended in front to clear space. He knew she would be upset. They'd already had the talk about him hanging out at the bar while she worked, and he knew he was only supposed to pick her up when she got off.

40

But after the beers, he knew if he went home, he would crash and probably not hear the phone.

A small space by the brass rail separating the waitstaff from the customers opened, and he slid into it. The bartender working the service bar spotted him and nodded, bringing a beer on his next trip. Will stood and watched the crowd; the packed dance floor was indistinguishable from the rest of the place, as everyone seemed to be moving to the beat of the band playing on the far side of the building.

Sheryl spotted him on her next trip to the bar, her face gleaming with sweat and her look exasperated. In line behind another server at the bar, she took a minute to talk before collecting her drinks and heading back out. "Will, what are you doing here?"

"I had a few at a bar by the job. Figured if I went home I would crash, so I came down here." No harm in the truth; she had a way of finding things out, anyway.

She threw a look at him, her green eyes that he loved so much now dark with anger. "You shouldn't be here."

The waitress in front of her moved away, her tray full of drinks, and Sheryl filled in her spot. The bartender leaned over and took her order.

"Please don't get drunk. Last time I almost got fired."

He knew he had been out of line before, but she had been right there with him. It was the night the bank had finally foreclosed on his house in the Keys. The last of all the last-ditch efforts to save it had failed, starting him on a binge that he had not quite emerged from. That night had been the worst. He had come to pick her up from a day shift, and they'd stayed late into the night drinking. He couldn't really remember much more than being escorted out.

Will turned away from her, thinking about leaving, but she would be off work in an hour. He could nurse the beer until then, probably have to listen to a rant on the way home, and then it would be over. Maybe he could use some of the money in his pocket to buy her a car. That would take a lot of the stress off their relationship. That word again stuck in his head, he turned away from the bar, contorting his body to avoid the guy behind him and lifting the beer over his head.

The guy moved forward to take his spot at the bar, and knocked Will off balance.

"Shit, you asshole!" screamed the girl next to him as he grabbed her to stop his fall, his beer splashing her face and dripping into her cleavage. "What the fuck are you doing?"

The man next to her stepped between them and pushed Will towards a waitress just leaving the bar who spilt her tray of drinks and screamed loud enough to attract the attention of one of the bartenders, who made a motion toward a bouncer. Inside of thirty seconds, Will had his arm cocked behind his back and was being paraded out the front door. He walked quickly from the bar, hoping that Sheryl hadn't seen him, but a second later she was on the sidewalk yelling his name.

He didn't turn around.

Chapter 6

Will's forced his eyes open, and shifted in the truck seat, spilling the last ounce of tequila from the pint bottle on his lap. His phone, long ago turned off, sat on the seat next to him. He wiped his face with his shirt sleeve and tried to put some reality on his situation.

The texts had started an hour after he left the bar—a stream of *How could you* turned into *You asshole* after he didn't answer. Finally, he had just turned it off. With nowhere else to go, he had parked in front of the fish house.

He got out and went toward the cooler, its shiny new lock catching his eye as he passed. Behind the box, the view was obstructed, and he relieved himself. Head banging, he went toward the hose, coiled up from yesterday, took off his shirt, and doused his head. His fingers combed through his hair as he emerged into daylight and looked around, trying to figure out where to start. The For Sale sign on the sailboat caught his eye as he put his shirt back on, and his recently single status cut through the haze of alcohol, giving him an idea.

Why not buy the boat and stay out here? That was more his style.

His stomach grumbled, and since it was too early to call about the boat, he made a material list and headed for Home

Depot, the only supplier open on Sunday, thinking maybe he could get some work done today if he kept the noise down.

* * *

Will sat in the restaurant, drinking his second cup of coffee, the empty plate pushed to the side. He sucked in his breath as he turned on the power to the phone, wincing as the onslaught of texts and voicemail messages from Sheryl bombarded him. It was easy to delete the voicemails, but fragments of the texts caught his eye as he tried to delete them before he could read them — and none of it was good.

Finally the screen showed no messages or voicemails. He fished in his pocket for the paper with the phone number of the boat owner, entered it into the screen, and hit dial. Several rings were followed by a grunt. It was almost ten, but apparently he had woken the owner. He almost hung up, but figured sailboats were hard to sell, and his call would be welcome.

"Hey, I saw the sign on your boat at the Pass-A-Grille Marina."

The voice changed from gruff to welcoming. "That's right, are you interested?"

"I am. Can you give me some details?" Will asked him about the size, sail inventory, condition, and engine. He also inquired what the dock fees were at the marina. They agreed to meet in an hour, and Will quickly shut the power off and put the phone in his pocket. He finished his coffee, paid the check, and left the restaurant.

Back in the truck, he planned out his bargaining strategy. Sailboats weren't the movers that power boats were, and this guy was paying a hundred and fifty-five a month to dock the boat there. He was sure to be motivated, though it was a good deal at the twenty-four hundred he had listed on the sign. Will was sure he could get him to two thousand.

He drove back to the fish house with a smile on his face. He knew it wasn't practical, but the thought of owning a boat again felt good to him. Maybe he could take it on a sail this afternoon, put out a handline and catch something. The lot was empty when he pulled in and he walked to the boat to wait for the owner. Just as he arrived, a head emerged from the cabin.

"You Will?" the head asked.

"Yeah. Can I take a look?"

The man showed Will the boat, started the engine, and went through the sails and controls. Everything seemed in order, and Will offered him eighteen hundred to get the negotiations going. They went back and forth, finally agreeing on twenty-one hundred and the rest of the month's dock fees the owner had already paid.

Will counted out the money from his dwindling supply and took the keys to the cabin. He was on his way to the marina office to change the name on the paperwork with the title in hand, when he saw a car pull into the lot. Sheryl got out of the passenger seat and went to the trunk. She opened it, took out a bag and a few boxes, and set them carelessly next to his truck.

Feeling euphoric after the boat purchase, he went toward her. "Can we talk?" he asked as he approached.

She turned to look at him, dropped the box she was carrying, and went toward him.

This was not the greeting he had hoped for, the look on her face telling him it had been a mistake to confront her. "I can explain."

Her eyes bored into him. "I had to plead for my job after what you did. I thought we agreed that you weren't going to hang out there while I was working."

"Please listen for just a minute, then you can go. I just turned around and the guy next to me knocked the beer into the girl. That's all. It was like dominos after that."

"Will, you don't get it. If you weren't there, it couldn't have happened. Can't you understand that?"

"I understand that you want me to do whatever you say to do. I can't have my life run like that. Maybe I should just stay here for awhile."

"Where are you going to stay?"

"I got that boat over there." He pointed to the slip.

"You got a boat. Of all the irresponsible things you could do. Will, you can't be thinking about yourself all the time. The money you spent on that," she pointed to the sailboat, "could have bought another car. Now what am I supposed to do?"

He hadn't thought about that. If this was what getting divorced was like, he wanted nothing to do with marriage. The remaining cash was still in his pocket. Out of guilt or some obligation, he wasn't sure, he pulled out the cash, took a couple of hundreds off the top and handed the rest to her. "This is all I have. Take it."

She didn't hesitate.

He took one last look at her, wondering if he was doing the right thing. It wasn't her fault things had imploded in the Keys. Her green eyes stared blankly at him; their previous fire having died out. Would life be better without her? He didn't know, but the way things were, he couldn't continue.

"Goodbye," he said as he walked away. He felt her there, even without looking, and knew exactly the pose she would be in. When he reached the seawall and set foot on the dock, he heard a car door slam. Seconds later, he turned around and the lot was empty.

He breathed a sigh of relief, went back to the building to pick up his belongings, and took them to the boat.

* * *

The sun was high in the sky and a glance at his phone confirmed it was just past noon when he decided to take the boat out. By the way the palm trees swayed in the breeze, he judged the wind to be about ten knots. Just right for an easy sail to check things out. He boarded the boat and started the mental checklist of the tasks he needed to perform. The five-gallon gas tank was full, and he figured with the small 20hp outboard, that would last about five hours if he needed it. He topped off the fresh water tank and checked the bilge. The engine started on its first pull, and he let it idle while he readied the dock lines.

The large marina building shielded the boats from the sea breeze, allowing him to let the lines go and put the engine in reverse without taking extra precautions. The boat slid out of the slip and turned as he moved the tiller toward the open water of the intracoastal waterway. Once clear of the marina, he followed the markers out Pass-A-Grille channel. The wind was directly in his face as he ran parallel to Shell Key. A string of boats were either pulled on the white sand beach or anchored just off of it. The only access to the pristine island was by boat, making it a more exclusive spot than the crowded public beaches around the point.

Clear of the last marker, he steered into the wind, let out the main sheet, and pulled on the main halyard to raise the mainsail. The sail luffed while he made his way back to the cockpit, shut the engine off, and changed course to two hundred seventy degrees—a bearing that would put him on a close haul. The boat took the wind and heeled slightly as he released the jib furling line and pulled out the jib sheet. The boats speed increased quickly with both sails up, and the sat on the high side of the boat, tiller in hand, watching the green water slip underneath him.

The water started to turn a darker, reminding him of the color of Sheryl's eyes this morning. He tried to put her out of his mind as he tacked back and forth, staying close to the two hundred seventy-degree bearing, timing the tacks so they were equal, in order to stay on course. Birds were circling off in the distance, and he made a note to bring a rod and reel, or at least a hand line with him next time. He judged the sun to be about halfway between its apex and the horizon when he tacked for the last time and brought the boat around slowly to a reciprocal bearing of ninety degrees. He was on a run now, wing on wing; the jib and main on opposite sides of the boat. With the tiller lashed in place, his mind drifted as the wind pushed the boat back toward land.

Suddenly a wave jarred him. He must have nodded off, easy to do with the boat rising and falling in the following seas. Suddenly alert, he scanned the horizon for the offending boat. Still about two miles from land, there was no need to run this close to another boat in the open waters of the Gulf. The afternoon was fading fast and there were several vessels making their way toward the pass, but the offending boat was easy to spot. Its unique cabin stood out on the speed boat.

The other boat was about a mile from the first channel marker, where it would have to reduce speed. He was curious, wanting to see if they were bringing in another catch. With his motor in addition to the sails, he figured he could catch it in the channel. A few minutes later, the Red #4 marker slid by his starboard side and he saw the fishing boat's silhouette against Sand Key. The sails were now a disadvantage as the other boat was stopped, possibly anchored to blend in with the other boats, probably waiting until dark to offload their catch.

Without knowledge of the channel, he was reluctant to lower the mainsail. To accomplish that maneuver, he would have to turn the boat into the wind before he could safely drop the sail. Instead, he decided to ease the main all the way out and pull in the jib. He grabbed the line for the roller furling in one hand and, leaving two turns around it for friction, took the jib sheet off the winch. Everything ready, he pulled in on the line for the roller furling and met only resistance. Checking the jib sheet, he realized that it wasn't the problem. The roller furling must be jammed. Concerned now, he tugged on the line several times, but the furling wouldn't budge.

He looked up to check on his progress and realized he was in trouble. The boat had just passed the 7B marker, and was hemmed in a narrow channel. With no options, he let both sheets loose, dumping the wind from them. The only problem was that he was running directly downwind, and the sails still powered him forward. He tried the engine next, turning the throttle to its max, but the small engine didn't have enough power to correct his course.

The boat was now dangerously close to the sand bar protecting Shell Key, and he was out of options. He tried to put the engine in reverse, but it was too little too late, and the keel of the boat ground into the sand.

He gunned the throttle in full reverse, trying to keep the keel from digging deeper, but a gust of wind drove the boat hard aground. Now, with a crowd of spectators moving toward him, he had to get the sails down. He released the halyard and let the main sail drop into the water, then climbed forward to release the jib.

He breathed deeply now that the damage had been mitigated and gathered the fallen sails in, then sat in the cockpit, wiping the sweat from his eyes. The tide would be high in a few hours and probably float him off the sand bar, but until then he would suffer the embarrassment of being gawked at by every boat entering the pass. Several came over to offer assistance, but in the tight channel, and confident the tide would soon do the work, he declined.

An hour later, as the sun was about to drop below the horizon, he was startled awake as the boat moved slightly. It was too early for the tide, so he assumed it was the wake of another boat. He looked up and saw the fishing boat staring bow on at him, the looming figure of Greg concealing the wheel house.

"Yo, contractor boy. Having some trouble?"

Will tried to ignore him, but the boat remained. "I'm good." Before he could wave him off, a line hit his deck. He looked at the boat and saw a bright orange bathing suit concealing very little of a tan body on the deck. His gaze remained there until Greg spoke.

"Bury your pride and let me pull you off. Can't have you sitting out here all night."

The last thing Will wanted was Greg's help, but he obviously wasn't going to go away. He went forward and tied the line to the stern cleat and signaled Greg to pull.

The initial thrust caught him off guard and he fell to the deck, thinking Greg had done it on purpose. His guess was confirmed when he looked at the other boat and saw the big man laughing from the helm as he backed his boat away from the sand bar. The water turned brown from the silt he kicked up, but the sailboat started to move.

Chapter 7

Will paced the floor of the fish house. It was almost nine, and the boys still hadn't shown up. He hoped they were coming, but the thought crossed his mind that Sheryl had called them off. He cursed himself for not getting their phone numbers, thinking they had probably partied late and just needed a wake up call. Irresponsible for sure, but he remembered when he had been their age, and if he weren't going fishing he was sleeping in. He stepped outside for the fourth time in the last hour to see if they were there, and looked at the yellow foam panel strapped to his truck. Early this morning he had taken a quick inventory of his depleted funds and made a plan.

The job relied on having a stable surface to work under the structure. On land this would have been easy, using scaffolding and planks, but in the water what he needed was a large floating platform, and that was where the foam panel came in. The four-by-eight sheet of twelve-inch polyurethane would support an elephant.

Looking again toward the street, he turned away frustrated. It would be harder alone, but he had done it for years and there was some work he could do without help. He went back to the truck and removed the panel, which was light enough to carry to the seawall by himself. After he glued and screwed a sheet of plywood to the top of the foam to protect it, he had to strain to push it into the water. It floated well as he boarded it for its maiden voyage.

Tentatively, he stood on the plywood deck, testing it for stability. He was just able to reach the floor framing under the building and he pulled himself along using the wooden joists as he test-drove the raft around the structure. Happy with the results, he went back to the seawall and hopped off.

There was still no sign of the boys. Resigned to work alone, he assembled his tools and some lumber. Back under the building, he went to the first hole and tied the platform to the closest pier with a dock line taken from the sailboat. A floor joist ran right through the center of the hole where he intended to place the new pier. This would have to be cut away and headed off with double joists, to support the load when he removed it.

He picked up the dangling end of an extension cord dropped through the hole, plugged his saw in, and started to cut away the joists at each opening. It was over an hour later when he finished and went back to the seawall.

The next hour was spent installing the boards he needed to reinforce the joists he had cut. Now he needed help to set the poles, but the boys were still not here. With no alternative, he changed plan and decided to jack up the structure around the first hole. This would normally be done after the pole was set and before the beam was installed, but there was no harm in doing it now.

It was already late morning when he loaded the platform with dive gear, some tools, a steel plate, a jack, and several pieces of six-by-six to use as temporary posts and pushed off the seawall. It was pleasant working underneath the building, much cooler than inside. The only disturbance was the small wakes from the boats passing by on the intracoastal waterway. He tied the platform off and started to get ready.

His original plan had called for one of the boys to be on the platform to help plumb the support post, but he thought if he took it slowly, he would be able to do it himself. Over the years, he'd preferred to work alone, devising ingenious ways to handle two-man jobs by himself. Now he'd just have to do the same. Before he geared up, he dropped the steel plate in the water and attached a plumb bob to the center point of the old beam. He had realized the standard carpenter's tool was too light and would be affected by the current, so instead he tied a four-pound dive weight onto a piece of nylon twine and dropped that. The weighted line would tell him where to center the plate underwater.

He suited up in a three-mil wetsuit for protection, and because he might be spending significant time in the water. Weight belt strapped in place, he shrugged into his BC, buckled the straps, and swung his right hand around his back to retrieve his regulator. He took a quick breath to confirm the air was on and placed the mask on his face. He side rolled off the platform and into the water.

Visibility was low as the current stirred the shallow water. The depth was only six feet here, and even the smallest tidal change would decrease visibility. When he was about four feet under, the bottom appeared; a mixture of sand with small rocks. He found the string line swaying in the current and worked to center the steel plate where the weight had landed. The plate was two feet by two feet, with angle iron welded in the shape of a square into the center to hold the post from sliding out. He surfaced and reached for the cut piece of six-by-six he would use to enable him to set the jack above the water line. With a hammer, he descended with the piece of wood, fighting its buoyancy as he tried to get one end to set on the plate.

Wishing he had chosen to spend the extra money on steel posts, he struggled with the surprisingly buoyant wood. Once set, he awkwardly hammered two nails into it to secure it in place. The experience of hammering a nail under water was unusual, the water buffering the hammer's effectiveness and accuracy.

Finally he surfaced, climbed onto the barge, and slid out of his dive gear. The rest of the work could be done above water. The ten-ton bottle jack fit on top of the six-by-six, and he measured to the beam, cut another section of post, and was ready. Hammering two toe- nails to hold the post to the beam, he set the jack in the space between the posts and started to work the handle.

The neck of the jack rose slowly, soon creating pressure between the two posts. When the jack met resistance, he slowed down, checking the posts for movement. If one of them got cockeyed with this much pressure, it could kick out with enough force to injure anyone in its way, and possibly damage the structure above. It would have been safer to have two men at this juncture; one to watch the level of the post and the other to work the jack.

Slowly, he pushed on the handle, listening to the building creaking as the weight was shifted. After an inch, the resistance became stronger. He would need a longer jack handle to create more leverage, but didn't want to take the time to get out of the water and find one, so he braced himself and pushed down hard on the handle.

* * *

"He's gonna fire us," Kyle said as he pulled into the lot.

"The dude's desperate. When was the last time you had a boss that talked that nice to you?" Dick replied as he took the last hit on the pipe. He held his breath before letting the smoke out. "Besides, we tell him a story about the car breaking down or some shit, and he'll buy it."

"If you didn't have to stay out 'till three partying, we could have been here on time."

"What are you, my mother? You were right there with me."

They pulled next to Will's truck and got out.

"It's hotter than seven hells," Kyle said as they went for the open door. Noise came from under the building as they entered, and he called out for Will.

Suddenly a loud pop sounded and the building vibrated.

"What the hell was that?"

"I heard a splash. Come on."

They ran outside to the seawall and looked under the building. The platform was still there, with one end of a broken beam laying on it. Will was nowhere in sight.

"He must be in the water," Kyle said as he jumped in. Dick followed, and they swam to the platform.

Dick took a deep breath and dove, surfacing a second later. "Can't see anything." He spotted Will's mask on the platform, put it on, and dove again. With a hand on the broken beam, he pushed himself to the bottom and started to look around. The silt was thick from the beam falling, and he could barely see his hand in front of his face.

Then something grabbed at his arm. It was Will, and he reached for him, but something was wrong. Unable to pull him up, he had to fight off Will's grip and surface. "He's down there," he yelled to Kyle and looked around. "Give me that rope."

With one end of the dock line in hand, he dove again. Will's hand grabbed him, though the grip wasn't as strong as it had been only seconds before. Dick worked frantically, using his hands to feel see what was trapping the body. Fighting the pain in his chest as his breath started to run out, he found the downed beam and looped an end of the rope around it.

"Pull!" He broke the surface and yelled at Kyle, then took another breath and submerged, not waiting to see if he understood.

Will felt lifeless when he reached him. He planted his feet on the bottom, grabbed him by his shirt, and pulled as hard as he could. When he was almost standing, he felt the weight come easily. Kyle must have pulled the beam off. Now free, he pushed Will to the surface, toward Kyle's waiting hand.

Will spat and coughed as they pulled him onto the platform. His eyes opened slowly.

"Give him some room," Dick said.

Will sat up slowly and looked around.

"He's not right. Let's get him up top," Kyle said.

They released the line holding the platform and pushed it toward the sunlight. Once at the seawall, Will tried to get off, but fell back.

"Easy, dude. We'll help you," Dick said. It took both of them to stabilize the floating foam enough to move Will onto the seawall where all three leaned back and collapsed.

* * *

They sat on the sidewalk eating lunch. Will was shaken, but feeling better. At least the beam hadn't hit his head. He knew he was lucky the boys had walked in when they did or he probably would have drowned.

"I want to have a look under there and see what happened."

"You sure that's a good idea?" Dick asked.

"We didn't know there was a danger factor built into this job when we signed up. Maybe we should be getting more money," Kyle added.

"Just be happy you still have a job. I was ready to fire you until you saved me there," Will replied. He was still upset that they were late; if they had been on time, one of them would have been down there with him. The accident may still have happened, but he would not have been alone. "Let's finish this up and have a look. One of you guys can be up top and one with me."

They finished eating in silence and went back to work. Will asked Dick to stay topside, and took Kyle underneath the building with him. They cleared off the platform and started to work their way back to the broken beam. The wood was split in two, now, with both ends submerged. One piece was short enough to lift without getting in the water.

Will backed off and called up through the hole. "Dick, find that dock line and send one end down. It'll be easier for you to pull it from up there."

A minute later, the line was through the hole. Will looped it around the end of the beam and called up to Dick to pull. All three lifted—Will and Kyle from below, and Dick from on top. The end came up easily now, and they maneuvered it onto the barge.

When Will saw it, he shook his head. It was rotted through. The complexity of the job had just increased tenfold.

Chapter 8

"Hey, can you give us an advance?" Kyle asked.

"You guys have only worked eight hours between Saturday and this afternoon." Will was almost out of money after giving most of the cash to Sheryl and buying materials—and the boat.

"Just a hundred each," Dick said. "That ain't gonna break you."

Will didn't need to check how much cash he had to know that it wasn't enough to pay them. He needed to get a couple of poles set, then he could ask Lance for another draw. But even that was going to be tough. Lance had been argumentative when he had called after finding the rotten beam. Will had offered to show him around and explain what would need to be done now, but he declined.

Silence had prevailed when he asked for more money. He explained how the rotten beams would also have to be replaced and that the job was bigger than he'd realized, and would take more time and materials.

Lance blew, starting to yell about time and costs and lost opportunity. How he was under pressure to get the job done now and that Will was only delaying the process to make more money.

Will had been confused first at his silence and apparent lack of concern to get the job done right. And then at his rant. But he could not overlook faulty work, and things were getting worse every time he turned around. Lance had changed overnight. He thought he had been hired to do the job right, not fast and cheap. He wasn't the right guy for that.

The noise of a loud truck interrupted his thoughts and he looked toward the road. Greg drove by, the truck slowing as he approached, clearly checking out the job; reminding Will that he was watching.

He looked back at the boys. "Listen, I spent just about everything on materials this morning. If we can get a couple of poles set, I can get some cash from the owner and pay you."

"How long's that going to take?" Dick whined.

The truck had turned around and was coming back toward them now, and Will couldn't help but glance at the blond hair flying from the open window. Even from this distance, she was breathtaking.

"Dude, seriously, that bitch is way over your head. And what about Sheryl?" Dick asked.

"We had a fight yesterday." Will looked back at the truck, hoping to catch one more glimpse of her, then turned back to Dick. "If we can get everything set up today, we can set the poles tomorrow, and I can get you cash on Wednesday."

"That's no good," Kyle said as he glanced at Dick.

Will watched the boys, noting the desperate look on their faces.

* * *

Dick and Kyle were alone in the boat house. Will had taken the platform underneath to inspect the other beams for damage. Kyle was drilling pilot holes through the plywood in each corner of the squares. Dick following behind him with a Sawzall to cut out the wood. After finishing two holes, Dick motioned Kyle outside.

They stood in the shade cast by the cooler. "Dude, we don't

get some money tonight, or we're freakin' dead. That dude's been waiting two weeks already," Dick said as he packed a bowl, lit the pipe, and pulled hard.

"Dude, if we hadn't partied last night we would have had it. Now what?"

"I thought we could get an advance out of Will and make everything cool. And there's no way the dickhead at the club is going to give us a cent. Maybe we should ask Sheryl." He took another hit on the pipe.

"We can ask, but we need a backup plan. That dude said eight o'clock. That's not a lot of time."

"Shit. What are we going to do? Remember those goons he sent after us last time we were this late? I thought they were going to hammer us, but they were cool, then. It'll be worse this time."

"You could stop smoking that shit. That'd be a start," Kyle said.

Dick dumped the spent contents on the pavement and put the small pipe back in his pocket. He leaned against the cooler. "Hey, what about the fish?"

"What fish?"

"In the cooler, idiot. Who's been smoking what?"

Kyle went around the side and looked at the door. "It's got a new lock."

"And how was that a problem last time?"

He shook his head. "I don't know."

"What the fuck? If there's something in there, it'll easily cover what we owe. We can take it to Dirk. Ground up in his fish spread no one will know it's illegal. And you know he won't care."

"Don't you think the dude that owns the cooler is going to come after us?"

"What's he gonna do, go to the police or something?" Dick started to pace. "First we gotta get Will out of here. Then we can check it out."

They walked back into the building, where Dick picked up the Sawzall and looked at the blade, mangled from the angle of the cuts he had made. He pulled the trigger and the saw buzzed. Watching the blade wobble back and forth while it oscillated, he got an idea. On his knees, he went to the next cut, stuck the blade in the pilot hole, and turned on the saw. Instead of easing it into the wood, he pushed as hard as he could. The saw hummed as the blade jammed and then snapped.

Dick looked at Kyle with a smile on his face.

"Hey, Will." Dick stuck his head in one of the holes and scanned the underside of the structure.

"Yeah?"

"Dude, sorry, but I broke the blade," Dick said. "You got any more?"

He waited while Will made his way back to the hole. "There's a bag over there with some. There's only a couple left in it, so you'll have to be careful."

"Oh, I will," Dick said as he went for the bag. He used the Allen wrench attached to the cord to change the blade. He needed to be patient, not something he was good at. It would be too suspicious to break them too quickly, but he needed to get Will out of the way so he could check out the cooler. He bent over the next hole and started to cut. This time the saw jerked in his hands as it hit an unseen obstruction, and the blade snapped. With two blades left, he replaced the broken blade and finished cutting through the nail.

Again the blade bound and broke.

With one blade left now, he was more cautious, but it soon found another nail.

"Hey, Will. That was the last blade!" he yelled through the hole.

"Just a minute," replied Will.

Dick waited by the seawall for Will to come over, and

helped secure the platform while he hopped off. "Bad luck, man. I kept hitting nails or something."

"That'll do it every time. I should have known, and bought the big pack. Why don't you guys take a break. I'll run to the store."

Dick smiled as Will went to his truck, started the engine, and took off. As soon as the truck was out of sight, he went into the building. "Kyle, he's gone. Grab those bolt cutters and let's do it."

He waited at the door for Kyle, who tripped crossing the threshold. Dick grabbed the cutters from him and went for the cooler door.

"Keep a look out."

The lock parted easily, the steel shank no match for the large cutters. Dick pulled it off, anxious to see what was inside. He opened the door and turned on the light. "Kyle! You gotta see this."

Kyle stood next to him, looking at the floor. Sitting on a tarp was the largest fish they had ever seen. Both boys had grown up by Tampa Bay, and still fished its waters for redfish and snook, but the fish covered the entire floor.

"It's a tuna," Kyle said.

"No shit, idiot. It's a goddamned bluefin. They get like twenty bucks a pound for these." Dick stare at the five foot long fish shaped like and overinflated football. If this fish weighed what he thought it did, and the math in his head was right, it was worth a pile of cash, there was no way he was selling it to Dirk.

"How are we gonna move this sucker?" Kyle asked.

"Okay. Give me a minute and let me think." He pulled the pipe from his pocket and lit up. After two puffs he handed it to Kyle, who declined. "We got to move it and replace the lock. We've probably got till dark before whoever it belongs to comes looking for it. This is a felony fish, and no question, they're not going to move it in daylight. Help me drag it to the edge. We'll tie it down underwater. Then you can take the car and get another lock. That ought to put the dude off for a while, thinking he lost the key."

They both grabbed the tarp and pulled. Expecting more resistance, Kyle stumbled, as the tarp slid easily against the cold metal floor. Once outside, it was another matter as they tried to drag the fish to the seawall. The tarp tore on the gravel and they were stuck, the fish too slimy and heavy to lift by hand. Dick started pacing anxiously, desperate to find a way to move the behemoth before Will came back, or worse. Kyle went back into the building and returned a few minutes later with three pieces of pipe.

"What the fuck man?" Dick was getting really anxious now, and wanted another hit on the pipe, but there was no time.

"Relax. They built the pyramids like this. Seen it on the History Channel." Kyle took a piece of pipe and, with Dick's help, slid it under the fish. "It'll roll now. I'll push it and you get ready with the next pipe. We can keep it moving if you stay one pipe ahead."

Dick nodded his head and waited with a section of pipe as Kyle started to push the fish. The slimy body tried to slide sideways across the smooth pipes, but other than having to direct the fish, it worked well.

"Now what?" he asked after the fish was at the seawall.

Again Kyle went into the building. This time he came back with a dock line. He took the preformed loop, slid the end of the line through it, then looped it over the fish's tail.

"Saw that on TV too?" Dick asked.

"Yup." Kyle went into the water and tied the line to a pier under the building. Back on shore, they both struggled to push the fish over the seawall. It landed with a huge splash, and they looked around quickly to see if anyone were watching. They stood for a few minutes mesmerized as the fish rolled under the building and out of sight.

"Come on, I'll clean this up. Take the old lock and get a new one just like it. There's a hardware store down the street."

* * *

Will was sure he had passed Kyle as he drove down Gulf Boulevard toward the fish house, but he shrugged and turned his mind back to his own problems. He had used his best sales pitch to get Lance to set up an account by credit card at the lumber yard on US 19.

He pulled into the parking lot and saw a suspicious movement out of the corner of his eye. Just as he got out of the truck, he saw Dick walk quickly from around the cooler. Something wasn't right; the boy was sweating and wet from the neck down.

"What are you doing?" he asked.

"Oh nothing, man. Just had a ride on your surf board thing down there. Thought I'd check it out while Kyle went to get us something to eat. Kind of lost my balance and fell off."

"No problem,. He handed him the bag with the large package of blades "Hey, can you show me how to cut through those nails without breaking these things?" Dick asked, and walked into the building.

Will followed. "I bought two kinds—one for metal and one for wood."

He wondered if Dick was listening to him at all.

Chapter 9

"Dude, we gotta go." Dick looked around the bar, getting more paranoid by the minute. There was no guarantee the tuna would be there when they got back; large predators were known to roam the intracoastal waterway, looking for easy prey hiding under the docks and boats. If any one of them picked up the scent of the dead fish, it wouldn't last long. "Come on and finish your beer."

"Would you relax? I want my paycheck," Kyle replied.

Ybor City had a whole different vibe on weeknights. The club was mostly empty, with only a few customers at the bar and canned music playing over the sound system.

"That fish is our paycheck. Rucker said midnight. He was pissed, but gave us a few extra hours. What time is it?"

Kyle pulled out his phone and checked the screen. "Almost eight. We got time."

Dick was getting anxious, and the beer was doing little to calm him. He needed to get to the car and smoke a bowl. But this feeling was going to stay with him until they got the fish sold. If things were left to Kyle, they would be sitting here until closing.

"We don't have all night. By the time we drive there, cut it up, and bring it back, it's at least a couple of hours. Then we have to pay Rucker off. It's cutting it really close."

"All right, calm down." Kyle finished his beer and walked

over to the owner, who was hanging out by the waitress station, talking to Sheryl.

Dick watched as the man stared at Kyle as if he had no business interrupting his conversation, or what looked more like a pick-up attempt. Kyle stared him down until he acknowledged him. They exchanged a few words and reluctantly the man disappeared toward the back of the club. Kyle chatted to Sheryl while he waited. The man was back in a few minutes, and shot Kyle a nasty look before handing him two envelopes. Kyle took them and went back to their seats.

"Okay. Let's go."

They left the bar and went to the car parked a half block away. As soon as Kyle had pulled into traffic, Dick pulled his pipe out, stuffed the bowl, and lit it. He proceeded to take several hits before handing it to Kyle, who took a small one and handed it back. The car was filled with smoke by the time they got onto the Crosstown Expressway and headed south toward 275 and the Howard Franklin Bridge.

"You know the dickhead was trying to pick up Sheryl," Kyle said.

"What's that matter to us? She didn't fall for his line of shit, did she?" He turned the music down a notch, curious for the answer.

"She was eating the shit up, man. Think we ought to tell Will?" Kyle asked.

"None of my business." Dick was not the gossip guy. "We can set him up at work Friday night and show her how much of dickhead he really is." The employees at the club loathed the owner, and took any chance they got to make him look bad, especially with his lame pick up attempts.

"Cool. Hope she doesn't go out with him." Kyle turned the music up as a Grateful Dead song came on.

They crossed the bridge over Tampa Bay and entered St.

Petersburg. Kyle exited on 22nd Street and headed toward the beach. There was little traffic, and they were quickly at the fish house. The parking lot was dark, though the large security light hanging over the door of the marina next door gave a twilight feel.

Dick got out as soon as the wheels stopped rolling and ran to the seawall to make sure the fish was there. He breathed in relief when he saw that the line was still attached to the pier.

He needed the Sawzall to butcher the fish. The fish house door was locked and it looked like he'd have to get it the hard way. He got on the platform and pushed himself toward one of the holes in the floor, where he jumped for the opening. His hands grabbed the rough edges of the concrete, and he pulled with all he had. Once his chest cleared the floor, he relaxed and took a breath before finishing the maneuver. He pulled himself the rest of the way into the dark fish house and started to look for the Sawzall. The rough teeth on the blade caught his eye and he worried how badly it would mar the flesh, but there was no option. He dropped back onto the platform with the saw and an extension cord trailing behind him, and pulled back to where the fish was tied up. Kyle was waiting in the water with the line in his hand when they heard a truck pull up.

They froze in place. The door slammed, and they heard someone walking toward them. The steps stopped short of the cooler, where a flashlight reflected off the metal and into the water.

"Goddamned mother-f'ing son of a goddamned bitch," the man swore.

Dick scooted closer, staying in the shadows to have a look. The guy was fumbling with a keychain, trying several keys. He knew they wouldn't work, and started to snicker under his breath. The man smacked the door, went back to his truck, and pulled out of the lot.

"That was close," Kyle said as he came up beside him.

"I told you to hurry at the bar, now we've got no time." Dick hopped off the platform and went for the fish. "We've got to get this cut up and get out of here before he comes back." He hauled the fish toward the seawall. "You got any more Macgyver moves to get this up there?"

Kyle looked at the fish and shook his head. He looked around, and saw a rock pile underneath the building where the seawall ended. "We can drag it over there and cut it up on the rocks. I think I can move the car so we can use the headlights to see."

Dick started to pull the fish by the tail rope. It moved easily through the water, but when he got to the rocks, he faced the same problem as they had before.

"Hold on," Kyle said. "Snake the rope up to the parking lot."

He went back to the seawall as Dick climbed on the rocks and pushed the end of the rope through a small opening between the building and the rocks. A moment later, the car started, and he watched the headlights as Kyle drove toward him, backed close to the building and got out of the car. He took the rope and tied it around the bumper.

"Yell when it's good," Kyle called out, and went back to the car. He put it in forward, and Dick watched as the line came taut. It was going to damage the valuable flesh, but they were out of both time and options.

With a quick squeal of the tires, Kyle accelerated, pulling the fish onto the rocks. Several large pieces of flesh tore off as it came out of the water, but there was enough fish not to worry about scraps.

The car door slammed and Kyle was soon back at his side with the Sawzall. "You better keep watch. I'll cut it up."

"That dude comes back, we're both dead. Better let me help. I can use the platform and shuttle the meat to the car."

Dick nodded and pulled the trigger on the saw. The teeth of

the blade cut easily through the thick skin and flesh of the tuna as Dick hacked away at it. He knew the cuts were ragged and he was probably losing money by butchering it this way, but he also knew it had to be done, and now. With one side carved off the spine, he started to cut it into manageable pieces as Kyle loaded them onto the platform.

"I'll take this and be right back," he said as he pushed the platform into the night air. Reaching the seawall, he hopped off and started unloading the huge fillets onto the concrete. He was about to jump onto the wall when headlights flashed into the parking lot and the truck pulled in.

"Shit, Dick! He's back."

* * *

Will was in the cabin of the boat, cooking a fillet from a snook he had caught earlier in the afternoon. He had noticed an abundance of fish under the building when he had done his inspection the other day and knew from his years as a guide how any kind of structure acted like a fish magnet.

Unfortunately, his rods and reels were still at his old house, and he had no desire for another run in with Sheryl, so he'd decided on a more primitive method. From the convenience store down the street, he bought some twelve-pound test line, medium-sized hooks, and bait. Using the holes they had cut in the floor like an ice fisherman, he rigged a line to each hole, using a two-by-four spread across the opening to hold it in place. An unattended line would not hook nearly as many fish, but there was a way around that. To set the hook, he pulled back two feet of line and looped it with a rubber band attaching it to the two-by-four with a nail. Once the fish hit, it would take the bait and pull on the excess line. The rubber band would allow enough time and recoil for the fish to hook itself.

With the rigs set, he went to get some supplies, hoping

dinner would be at the end of one of the lines when he got back. Less than an hour later, when he returned, two of the rigs were pulled tight, the rubber bands broken. The lines came up easily, with a fat snook on the end of both.

That was two hours ago. He had filleted the fish and walked across the street to the beach to watch the sunset. Now back aboard, he had two fillets cooking in butter on the small gas stove. With dinner cooked, he went back to the cockpit to escape the heat of the cabin. But just as he sat down to eat, he saw the lights of the truck pull into the parking lot next door. He set the plate down, stepped onto the dock, and made his way to the seawall, As he got closer, he saw what looked like Kyle's car against the building.

Fearful that the boys had broken into the cooler again and were now in danger, he did a quick inventory of what was at hand, trying to find anything that might be serviceable as a weapon. He felt some responsibility for their indiscretion—unable to pay them earlier, they were probably desperate for cash. His tools in the fish house, so he ran back to the boat and looked through the storage compartments. A few minutes later, with a flare gun in one hand and a boat hook in the other, he crept back toward the building.

Greg was standing by the door of the cooler with two men, cursing under his breath as he tried several keys in the lock. He relaxed slightly as he realized that if the lock was intact, the boys must have been up to something else. Greg yelled something at one of the men, who went to the truck and came back with a pair of bolt cutter. The man returned, cut the lock and opened the door.

"It's gone!" one of the men yelled.

Greg looked around the lot. "What's with that clown car over there? It's running. Go find out who's here!" he screamed.

Will crouched low to avoid being seen as he watched the three men spread out and search. They tried the door to the building, but it was still locked. The beam of the flashlight moved to the seawall, and Will could clearly see Kyle standing chest deep in the water with a pile of tuna fillets.

There was nothing he could do as Greg yelled for the men. They pulled Kyle out of the water. One threw him against the building while the other loaded the fillets into one of several coolers in the back of the truck.

Greg went over to Kyle and punched him in the stomach. He started yelling questions at him, but Kyle just stood there, looking like he was going to throw up, and said nothing. One of the men came over to them and said something to Greg that Will couldn't make out. Greg punched Kyle in the face and went to the truck.

A moment later, he came back toward the shaken boy, his hands balled into fists. Will could clearly hear him screaming that it was only half the fish. He hit him again and Kyle went down in a lump. Then he kicked him and the two men dragged him to the truck.

Chapter 10

Will ran to the seawall the minute the truck pulled out of the lot. Both the platform and concrete were covered in blood and fish slime. He turned to look at Kyle's car, noticed it was still running, and went to turn it off. As he reached in through the open window to turn off the ignition, he saw a pair of eyes reflected in the headlights. His first thought was a gator, but they didn't live in salt water. Wondering what else it could be, he went to the gap between the building and the seawall.

"Will. What the fuck," came the broken voice.

"Dick? They're gone. Come out of there," Will said.

"I gotta get the rest of this fish out. Where's Kyle?"

"You didn't see?"

"No. I saw that dude pull up in the black truck, but that's it. Can you send the platform over here?"

Will went back to the corner of the building where the platform bobbed in the small waves, kicked some of the fish remnants into the water, and climbed on. As he started to pull the joists, he slipped on the greasy plywood, barely keeping his balance. He maneuvered his feet to a clean spot and pulled the platform toward Dick. The fish carcass lay on the rocks, a pile of rough-cut fillets beside it.

"Holy crap. Where did that come from?"

"Never mind that, I'll tell you later. Can you just get me out of here and tell me what happened to Kyle?"

Will could hear the panic in his voice, and decided to get him to the parking lot before telling him that Kyle was gone. He pulled the platform toward him and helped load the fillets. Dick jumped on next to the three huge piles of meat with the Sawzall in hand and a panicked look on his face. Seawater flooded onto the overloaded deck as Will pulled the craft toward the seawall. When he reached the end of the building, he glanced at the parking lot to see if there were any onlookers and, with a final push, escaped the confines of the understructure.

"You better start talking," Will said as he pulled his body from the platform to the seawall.

Dick sat next to the fillets. "Would you just tell me what happened to Kyle?" He got up, jumped onto the seawall and started pacing nervously,

"That guy, Greg, took him. Smacked him around and then threw him in the truck. Okay? Now spill it."

Dick started to balk. "We were just trying to get some cash to pay this guy back. If you would have given us the advance—"

Will blew. "Don't you even *think* about blaming this on me. You guys have known me for three days and worked all of eight hours. You make your own decisions."

"Okay, okay." Dick looked around. "Hey, you don't have any weed do you? My stuff is wet."

"Damn it, Dick. Kyle is gone, you have a pile of what looks like illegal bluefin tuna, and you want weed?"

"It calms me down. You have no idea." He put his head down.

"Would you please tell me what you two are into, and maybe we can figure out what to do about Kyle."

He was getting impatient. Greg could have killed him by now and dumped his body, or he could be coming back here to look for the rest of the fish. The more he thought about it, the more he realized the story could wait. If Greg *did* come back, and found them like this, he would be implicated as well.

"Hurry up. Let's get the fish in the building and clean this mess up before he comes back. Then we can figure out what to do about Kyle. It's not going to help him if we get caught, too."

They carried the piles of fish into the building, fighting the flies that were eagerly swarming around the warming fillets. Dick dragged a hose to the platform and cleaned the surface and seawall. When all the evidence was gone, Will took the platform underneath again. Swatting the flies, he jammed a large screwdriver into the eyes of the fish to keep it from floating to the surface, and then unceremoniously slid it into the water.

Dick was just finishing the cleanup when Will emerged and tied off the platform. "Let's go to my boat, and you can tell me what in the hell you two are into."

He walked away without waiting for an answer. Halfway down the dock, he saw Dick close the car door and come running after him. Back on board, he sat in the cockpit and waited while Dick told him about the cooler and the fish, stopping frequently to pull hard on a roach he must have recovered from the car.

"So, you guys broke in again? I guess it won't do any good to fire you." He got up.

"Where you going?"

"To the police. Your friend has been abducted and you're sitting here smoking a joint. It's not my problem, but someone has to do *something*."

"Wait. Look, man."

Will turned to walk away.

"Okay, there's more. Me and Kyle are in some trouble with some bad dudes. You can't go to the police. I've got a couple of bench warrants, and what about the fish? We stole it, too. It's his word against ours, and that's like felony shit."

Will turned around and sat down. He needed a few minutes to process all the information, and sent Dick into the cabin for two beers. The downside of taking this to the police quickly came to mind as he sipped his beer. Between the illegal fish and the abduction, the fish house would be a crime scene forever. There would be no more income from the job, and he had no other prospects.

He looked at Dick. Even though it had only been a couple of days, he had grown attached to the boys. He couldn't put his finger on it, but it seemed that there was a little bit of each of them in him, and they were starting to grow on him like younger brothers.

Plus, if he went to the police, he was probably also guilty by association. Then he would have to worry about retribution from Greg, as well as prison time.

"Okay. No police. For now. We know Greg has him, and I met a couple guys the other night that know him. I can go over to the bar where they hang out and talk them up. See if I can find out where he lives, or if he has any commercial buildings around here. Hang out — I'll be back."

He got up to leave, giving Dick a hard look before he acknowledged him.

* * *

Dick waited for a few minutes, finishing the joint and throwing it overboard before he got up and went back to the fish house. What was the point of sitting there waiting for Will, when the least he could do was to sell the fish and pay off his and Kyle's debt? The padlock on the plywood door was locked and he had a quick, anxious moment before he remembered the holes in the floor. He went back to the platform and pushed himself under the building, stopping at the first hole he came to. As he had earlier, he struggled through the opening, missing on his first attempt. Once inside the building, he went for the fillets, now covered with flies, and started tossing them down onto the platform. He followed the last one through the hole and pushed the platform toward the seawall.

With an eye on the road in case Greg or Will came back, he loaded the fillets into the backseat, rubbed his slimy hands on his cargo shorts, and sat in the driver's seat. It had been a while since he had driven, having lost his license to traffic violations and court no-shows a year or so ago, but the keys were still in the ignition and he started the engine. Flies buzzed around his head as he opened the windows and pulled out of the lot. Once on the road, he drove as fast as he thought he could get away with, the flies streaming out the windows as he accelerated.

The only choice to sell the fish now was Dirk, the fish dip guy. Dick figured he had at least a hundred pounds of fillets that would get him at least a couple hundred dollars—just enough to pay off Rucker. He knew the fillets were worth more, but he had no idea where to get their true value. He drove toward the Gandy Bridge, glancing down at the lights from the boats fishing below, and wishing he were there instead of in his current mess.

At the end of the bridge, he followed Gandy Boulevard for several blocks before turning right into an older residential area. He passed rows of homes, mostly built in the 40s and 50s, all with the same ranch house layout and shallow pitch roof. They'd been built to house the residents of the nearby Air Force Base. He stopped at a rundown house with an unkempt front yard. An old neglected boat sat on a trailer with a flat tire in the driveway. Even in the dark he could tell the lawn was dead.

A light came on as soon as he pulled in the driveway, and a face peered out from behind the flimsy curtains. Dick breathed a sigh of relief; Dirk must have recognized the car, because he went right to the door. They talked neighborhood gossip for a few minutes before Dick showed him the fillets. It had taken a few minutes of negotiation, but Dirk had seen the fish for what it was and paid him a premium.

A few flies still swarmed the slimy backseat as Dick pulled out of the driveway, but at least he had some cash. Enough to pay their debt and maybe score a little more weed to see him through.

He drove slow now, careful to stay just below the speed limit as the houses started to get nicer. The neighborhood changed from all older homes to a few blocks of old, mixed with newer homes, dwarfing the original houses. Builders had moved in and started buying the smaller homes, tearing them down and building as large a house as possible.

Soon all the houses were new and he checked his rear view mirror, expecting to see the lights of a police car. He approached a large house and pulled into a driveway, skirting the large circle in front of the house, and proceeded to a gate on the side, where an intercom buzzed. The gate opened in front of him. The smaller driveway led to a courtyard behind the home, where he parked and waited, knowing that Rucker had seen him on the security cameras.

"Dicky."

He heard the voice before he saw the man. The relationship tortured him. They had run in the same group in high school, but Rucker had cleaned up his act and gone to college, while Dick was, well, where he was. Rucker had become a banker, but his greed had grown, and he'd started supplementing his banking career with drug sales. The man approached the car, dressed in a high-class suit and smirking.

"Didn't expect to see you. And driving! Shit. Where's Kyle?"

"He's working."

"Well, you come to settle up?" He looked at his watch.

"Yeah, I got your money." Dick handed him several hundreds through the window.

Rucker took the money, folded it neatly, and put it in his pocket. "That's it? Where's the rest?"

Dick stammered, "Kyle said we owed five hundred. That's what I gave you."

"He didn't add the interest and penalty. You guys are real late. I need another two hundred." He leaned into the window. "Christ, what's that smell?"

Dick sat there frozen. Rucker might have been a high school friend, but he was serious about his side business and collecting. He had no qualms about sending muscle after his money. Dick handed him the extra hundred he had held back, hoping that would placate him.

"Another bill. That'll buy you another day. But remember, it goes up fifty a day."

Dick didn't answer. He pulled the shifter into reverse and backed into the turnaround, then put the car in drive and drove back toward the street. The gate was closed, and he had to wait anxiously for Rucker to open it before he could leave. He knew the guy had waited the few extra seconds before opening it just to torture him.

Two streets over, he pulled into a dark spot under a burnt out streetlight, and checked the glove compartment. There was a small baggie with a little weed—maybe enough for a day. But the way things were going, he knew his consumption was sure to go up with all the stress.

He reached into his pocket and pulled out the pipe, dumped the wet contents onto the street, and packed a full bowl. At least the ride back to the beach would be mellow, he thought as he turned on the radio.

Chapter 11

While Will walked to the bar, he thought about what to do. Kyle was in danger, and he wondered about his decision about the police. Maybe an anonymous tip would at least alert them there was a problem, but other than that, he could find no way to approach the authorities without involving himself and Dick.

Entering the bar, he looked around and saw one of the guys he had talked to the other night. They exchanged pleasantries and Will sat next to him, and turned his attention to the football game on the TV. It wasn't that he had any interest, he just didn't know how to break the ice. The men exchanged a few comments about the game as they watched and drank. Will finished his beer and summoned the courage to ask about Greg. There was really no way to ask what he needed without sounding like he was fishing for information, so he didn't attempt to disguise the conversation.

"You know that guy we were talking about the other night?" he started. "I need to find him. Do you know if he lives around here, or has an office or anything?"

The man put down his beer and looked Will in the eye. "I warned you about Greg and his crooked deals. You haven't gotten involved in something have you?"

"Not me. But a friend kind of got mixed up in something." He felt better not lying.

"All the same, even the police keep their distance from him. He actually filed a law suit a couple of years ago that they were harassing him. I don't know how it ended, but since then, he runs around the beach like he owns it." He drank from his beer. "Be careful, is all I'm saying."

He took a cocktail napkin off the bar and scribbled an address.

* * *

Dick snapped erect as the flashing lights came on behind him. He turned off the radio and tried to control his heart. As he started to pull over, the police car sped around him and accelerated. He was shaking so badly he had to pull off onto the shoulder, but after a few minutes, when he was calm enough to drive, he started the car, waited for a large gap in the traffic and accelerated.

As he crossed the reflectors and entered the right hand lane, he was greeted by the rough lumpy feeling of a flat tire. He pulled back to the shoulder, got out and went to the rear of the car. The rim rested on the pavement, with what little remained of the tire surrounding it. A quick kick brought pain to his foot and little relief. Hobbling, he went to the trunk and opened it. Surprised the spare was there and actually had air in it, he pulled it and the jack from the trunk and set to work.

Fifteen minutes later, he was back on the road. His hands still shook from the scare, and he checked his pocket for his pipe, which was gone. Somehow, he must have lost it when he changed the tire.

Now he was really anxious. He pulled over at the next exit and checked the glove compartment. There was still a small amount of pot left in the baggie, but he needed some now, and had no pipe or papers. He checked his pockets again, confirming what he suspected—that he was broke as well.

This was not a good situation for him. In fact, the first thing he checked every morning was that he had enough for the day, often rechecking several times during the day as well. He needed the weed.

A sign for a 7/11 down the street gave him an idea, and he pulled back on the road. He took the turn into the parking lot too fast, hitting the muffler on a bump. He parked and scrounged through the car looking for loose change, barely finding what he needed for a single beer. The clerk asked for ID and he had to settle for a soda. The beer would have served double duty, but the soda would serve his purposes.

Outside, he dumped it on the grass and used the key to puncture the round part of the can, where he fashioned a bowl. This would work for now. He got back in the car and moved to a dark spot in the abandoned lot next door, where he lit up and waited for the effects to calm him.

* * *

The man had left, and Will was alone at the bar, staring at the address written on the napkin and wondering what to do. He was not prone to rash decision, more apt to study a problem, evaluate it from all sides, and then jump off the cliff.

The bar door opened and he lost track of his thoughts, as the blonde from Greg's truck walked in and glanced around the room. It couldn't be any one else—he was sure of it. Her blond hair, backlit by the parking lot lights, was so fine it was almost translucent. His breath caught in his throat both from the sight of her and the probability that Greg would be walking in right behind her.

Unable to look away, he caught her eye and froze as he watched her come toward him.

"Hey, you're the guy from the construction job," she said with an eastern European accent. She pulled out the vacant stool and sat.

"Yeah," he muttered. Something was not right here. He looked toward the door, but it remained closed. Greg could be walking in any second, and he tried to distance himself.

But he kept glancing back at her. She sat at the bar with her head in her hands, and looked like she was crying. He sipped his beer and waited, not sure what to do. It didn't really matter whether he consoled her or ignored her, if Greg walked in and saw them sitting next to each other it was going to be bad either way.

Slowly her head came up and she looked at him. Tears streamed down her face, her mascara following in their tracks. He reached for a napkin and handed it to her.

She took it and wiped her eyes. The bartender walked toward them, tossing a quick glance at Will. Some kind of warning, he was sure, and then the three of them watched each other, not sure who would break the silence. Finally, the girl looked up and asked for a glass of wine. The bartender walked down the bar, grateful for the excuse, leaving them alone again.

"You okay?" Will asked, not knowing what else to say. Talking to girls in bars was not in his wheelhouse, especially this one, who had ties to Greg. He took another sip of his beer and looked away.

"Yeah, thanks for asking." Her accent sounded Russian, though he couldn't place it for sure.

The bartender was back, and set the wine glass down on the bar. He looked at Will as if he knew that he would be paying. Will nodded toward him and he walked away.

"Thanks. My name is Jazmyn," she said as she took a tentative sip and then downed half the glass.

He looked at her, knowing it was an alias, but enjoying the sound of it all the same. "Where's Greg?" he asked, glancing again at the door.

"Gregori? We got in a fight. He threw me out of the truck in front of this place. I don't have my money, ID, or anything." She started to sob again.

He glanced at her, not doubting that she had no money or ID; there was no place to put it. Her T-shirt and shorts were both low cut and tight. There was no room for any extraneous objects. Able to relax slightly, not having to worry about Greg barging through the door at any moment, he thought of another problem: He had no idea what to do. As if on cue, she took over the conversation.

"That bastard. I am done with him." She gulped the rest of the wine and looked at him.

He knew she wanted another. His feet started moving, knowing they should get him out of here, but his head told them otherwise. And then she stared at him, and he started to rationalize. A couple more glasses of wine and maybe she would give him some information about Greg—maybe something he could use to get Kyle back. He signaled to the bartender, knowing he was lying to himself, but unable to stop.

A fresh glass in front of her, she slid the stool closer, changing the spacing from what two guys would be comfortable with to the closeness of a couple. What now? His mind couldn't help jumping to places he knew it shouldn't be going. Sheryl was nowhere in his thoughts as he visualized them both on his sailboat.

* * *

Dick sat in the car and waited for his nerves to settle. He glanced at the pot left in the baggie and did some quick calculations. It didn't take long, and soon he was scooping the rest of the weed into the indentation he had made in the soda can and lighting it.

The smoke filled the small car as he exhaled. When the cloud finally cleared, after he had recycled as much of the smoke as possible, he realized he had just added to his problems. Without a supply of weed, he couldn't function. How was he going to get Kyle back and raise the rest of Rucker's cash sober? The thought frightened him.

Will was working the beach angle, and he didn't think there was much he could do on that front, besides get in the way. He had said he was not going to the police, but Dick couldn't be sure of that. With a handful of bench warrants out for him, he couldn't take the chance of them running his name.

May as well go back to Tampa, check out who was at the bar, and try and score some weed. If Will did get the authorities involved, he would at least be in another jurisdiction. Maybe that would give Will some time to find Kyle. He started the car and pulled out of the lot, noticing the gas gauge had less than an eighth of a tank.

With enough of a buzz to hold him, the twenty-minute drive to Ybor City went quickly. The street was quiet, and he pulled into a space in front of the bar. It was close to last call when he walked into the club and glanced over at the two barstools he and Kyle had been sitting on just a few hours earlier. The bar was crowded, mostly with regulars and employees hanging out on their night off. He scanned the crowd, hoping to see one or two friendly faces who might front him a bag until the weekend, but his glance stopped on Sheryl, who was sitting alone in a booth at the end of the room.

With nothing to lose, he walked over and looked at her.

"Hey, Dick."

"Hey," he stalled. "Hey, can I talk to you for a minute?"

"Sure. Get a beer and put it on my tab if you want. It's about last call. Get me one too."

She was slurring slightly, but he was not going to pass on a free beer. He went to the bar and came back to the table with two longnecks in hand, he stood awkwardly, waiting for an invitation to sit.

"You look like you've seen a ghost. Sit down."

Dick looked around, wondering why she was sitting alone, then remembered that the club owner had been hitting on her before.

She must have read his mind. "He's upstairs, cashing out a couple of waitresses. Probably won't be down for a while. Go ahead and sit."

He slid into the booth and passed her one of the beers, drinking deeply from his. His courage as high as it was going to get, he sat upright. "Will said maybe you could lend me some cash. Maybe 'till Friday."

She looked at him. "You know we broke up, right? I don't know what he's got going on over there. Buying sailboats and whatever."

Dick clenched his jaw and looked around the bar again. She was his only chance. "Okay. Never mind Will. How about fifty bucks 'til Friday? I'll pay you from the tips that night. Promise." He waited.

"I'll lend you the cash if you tell me what you were about to say earlier."

He gave her a questioning look.

"You know. When you saw me with the club owner. I could tell by the look on your face that you knew something. I haven't been around here that long, and he seems nice."

Dick was unsure how to continue. He couldn't afford to lose his job, but seeing Sheryl with the owner was too much for him. "Dude's a prick. Me and Kyle call him the dickhead. He picks up these girls and I don't know what happens, but some of them come back looking for him. Mad like shit."

She looked at her beer. "I guess I was hoping for the best, but I kind of had a feeling." She sucked down the rest of her beer. "I'll tell you what, you give me a ride home and I'll lend you the money."

Dick didn't need to be asked twice. He slammed the beer down and got up.

She must have caught his drift. "Let's get out of here before he comes back down. I didn't promise anything."

"Don't worry," Dick said, hoping this would not cost their jobs.

Chapter 12

Will knew he had to get his head on straight. The girl had gone to the bathroom, and he likely had a few minutes to get his head organized. Finding Kyle was the reason he was here; not to become bewitched by a Greg's girlfriend. He knew she was trouble, but that didn't change anything and again he couldn't take his eyes off her as she walked back to the bar. Forcing himself back on topic was not easy as she eased onto the bar stool, brushed her hair from her face, and finished her glass of wine. She looked at him again, and he nodded to the bartender, hovering nearby as if on cue.

"That guy you got in a fight with. Greg, right?"

"Gregori, yes." She nodded.

"Do you know where he lives or keeps his boat or anything?"

She nodded again and he waited for an answer. But the silence dragged on, the mention of Greg's name having changed her mood.

Suddenly he had an idea. "Do you live with him?"

Again she nodded.

"Maybe I can take you over there to get your stuff and you can stay on my boat for awhile. You know, until you get sorted out."

She looked at him and pursed her lips as if to speak. He

wasn't sure if she just didn't have the language skills to communicate, but she seemed to understand. Maybe she was fearful of Greg's retribution.

Just as he was about to give up, she murmured, "You have a boat?"

It wasn't much, but it was a start. "Yeah, a small sailboat. Kind of like camping." He didn't want to get her expectations up. "It's big enough for two, though."

"Maybe that would be a good idea. I don't think he'll be home. He was getting the boat ready when we fought. Looked like he was going to be out for a few days from the supplies he was loading."

"Cool. My truck is at the marina next to the fish house. We'll have to walk there."

"Okay. But can I have one more?" She finished the full glass of wine in two gulps. "Please?"

Will couldn't afford to drink here all night. "How about if we get a bottle on the way back."

He was excited. If Greg had gone out fishing, there was a chance that Kyle was in the house alone. He fingered the three bills left in his pocket, knowing his funds were in the extreme danger zone, and pulled a twenty out. The bartender came over and took it from his grasp, leaving him with two twenties.

Without a look back to see if there was enough left for a tip, he guided her from her seat and walked toward the door. Her high heel caught in the crack between two of the rustic floor boards, and he had to catch her. The contact electrified him, and he held her arm as they walked out of the bar into the humid night.

She struggled with her heels, but after a few blocks she took them off. As they reached the marina, he became anxious about the boat and his truck. Living with Greg, she was probably used to much better trappings than he had to offer. She didn't seem to hesitate as they got into his old truck. He started it up, backed out of the lot and looked to her for directions.

They went north on Gulf Boulevard for a few minutes, and she told him to make a right turn at Cabrillo Avenue. Again she pointed toward the right, and they entered a residential neighborhood with large houses on the left and a vast assortment of boats swinging from davits or tied to their docks across the street. She signaled him to pull over across from one of the larger houses, and he looked in dismay at Greg's truck in the driveway. Then relaxed as he remembered that she had said he was going fishing. He glanced to the right and realized the dock directly across from the house was empty.

Still on guard, he exited the truck and waited for her. She led the way up the driveway, but instead of going to the front door, she went to the side of the house, where she reached around the corner. He was about to ask what she was doing when the sound of the garage door opening distracted him. She came back around with a smile, and led him into the garage.

Epoxied black, the floor of the garage shone in the light of the overhead fluorescent lights. He looked around, noting that nothing was out of place until they reached the door leading to the house. As he was about to follow her in, he took his glance from her tight butt and noticed a pile on the floor next to the stairs. There was a T-shirt covered with what looked like blood and a few feet of rope. The shirt looked like the one that Kyle had worn that day. He started to take notice of his surroundings more as she led them through the house.

"I could use a bathroom. Why don't you get your stuff? I'll find you when I'm done."

He didn't wait for an answer before he took off the other way, down the hall to an open door. It was a bedroom, and looked unused. Quickly, he went to a window, released the lock, and slid it open an inch. If he needed to get back in, this would insure him entry. He moved through the house, quickly finding it empty until he reached the master bedroom, where Jazmyn was stuffing a bag.

She turned to him and walked toward the door, obviously expecting him to get the bag. He went to the bed and saw a handheld GPS on the dressing table. With a glance to the door to make sure she couldn't see, he grabbed the unit and shoved it in the pocket of his cargo shorts before grabbing the bag and following her.

They left the house through the garage, and he again glanced at the T-shirt. Maybe the GPS would give him an idea of where they'd gone. He reached the truck before she did and started the engine, anxious to get away, and hoping that phase two of his plan would work as well as phase one.

* * *

Will had a hard time thinking on the way back to the marina. Jazmyn pressed against him, her bag taking up the extra space in the front seat. He tried to concentrate, but her thigh brushing against him made any other thoughts impossible. There was little he could do tonight except plan, and his conflict became clear in his mind. Although he desperately wanted her, he would not be able to check the GPS unless he could get some privacy.

There was also the possibility that she had value to Greg; maybe he could trade her for Kyle.

His best bet right now was to put aside his lust and get her to sleep. Then he could have a look at the GPS. They were about to pull into the marina parking lot when the lights of a convenience store caught his eye.

"Wine?" he asked.

She nodded, looking bored.

"Okay. I'll be right back." He opened the door and left the car, wondering if he could get one of those big bottles for less than ten dollars. Avoiding the potholes, he crossed the lot and opened the door. The blast of expected AC never came, and the store was as humid as outside. Condensation covered the glass door of the refrigerated wine case, which he hoped was still working as he went toward it.

The big bottles were all around twenty dollars—way too much for his dwindling reserves. He turned to the smaller bottles and noticed a rack with single-dose medicine packets hanging from hooks. A six-pack of cheap wine coolers and a packet of NyQuil in his hands, he went to the counter and paid the clerk, who thankfully didn't ask about the combination.

He crossed the lot and got back in the car, trying to figure out a way to get her to take the pills. A few minutes later, they pulled into the marina. She followed him toward the dock where he extended his hand to help.

"Might want to take off your heels again."

She bent down and reached for her shoes, revealing her cleavage through a gaping hole in her blouse. He didn't recover as quickly as he would have liked, and she caught his eye as she straightened, but to his relief, she smiled. He turned and led her to the boat, offering his hand to help her aboard. She tripped over a cleat and ended up in his arms. As his arm grabbed her, he thought about delaying his plan.

"Hope the accommodations are okay," he said hopefully.

She didn't answer, but sat on the bench by the tiller, tossed her shoes onto the deck, and held a hand out for a cooler. He exhaled, twisted the cap off, and handed it to her. She took the bottle and rubbed it seductively between her breasts.

"It's hot," she whined. "No AC, I guess."

There was no good answer, and he was more aroused than he should be, so he unlocked the cabin door. Once inside, he put four of the coolers into the small propane refrigerator and opened one for himself. He looked out the companionway and watched her as she adjusted herself to get comfortable on the bench.

"I'll be right up."

No answer came. He reached into his pocket and took out the pills. With a knife, he cut them in half and squeezed the contents into the open cooler. The halved lemon he had used on the fish earlier lay on the counter, and he squeezed that in as well, hoping to cover the taste. With the cap screwed back on he shook the concoction, opened it, and took a sip, hoping after the first cooler, she wouldn't notice the taste, he replaced the cap, grabbed a cooler for himself, and went back on deck.

* * *

An hour and three coolers later, she was asleep on the bench. Will checked on her once more, to be sure, went into the cabin and sat at the small table. He adjusted the fan to hit his face, hoping he wouldn't drip sweat onto the papers spread out in front of him. A quick search of the cabin had revealed several charts as well as dividers and parallel rulers. With a carpenters pencil in hand, he started the GPS and waited for the unit to synchronize itself with the satellites it used to pinpoint position.

The unit took a few minutes to satisfy itself and the screen changed. He scrolled through the options and found the waypoint screen. There were forty-two waypoints, all but a few sharing similar coordinates. Starting with the first, he took the latitude and longitude for each, and plotted the coordinates on the chart, using the waypoint number to label the spot.

It took almost an hour to plot all the points. They were clustered around an area called the Middle Grounds by local fishermen and divers. The area was eighty miles into the Gulf of Mexico. A major trip, but the rewards, as evidenced by the fish the boys had found in the cooler, were worth it. With the dividers, he transposed the scale on the side of the chart placing one point on the marina and walking the other to the cluster of marks and measured the distance. Eighty-five miles confirmed his guess. Next he took the parallel ruler and lined one end up with the magnetic reading on the compass rose, and brought the other side to the line he had drawn. The course read 283 degrees, and he noted that next to the line.

He rolled the chart up, took the GPS to the forward berth, and put it in a small compartment he had found under the mattress. Then he went back out to check on Jazmyn. She was snoring softly, and he just stood there for a moment and watched her breasts rise and fall.

Chapter 13

The weather service prediction last night had been for the wind to blow fifteen knots, and that's exactly what Will felt as he stepped out of the cabin onto the dark deck. He could only hope the conditions held. Heading eighty miles offshore was a daunting task, especially when he was sailing single-handed, but he had no other ideas. The cluster of waypoints he had plotted on the chart last night were all within a few miles of each other. That was the most likely place to find Greg, and hopefully Kyle with him. As long as the wind stayed below thirty knots, he was comfortable with the trip. Anything over that and the seas would hit six feet, decreasing visibility and restricting his movement on the boat.

If something failed with the wind blowing, it would go wrong in a big way. The boat had a roller furling on the jib and a self-reefing mainsail that should allow him to decrease the sail area without leaving the cockpit — but the roller furling had already jammed once and the mainsail reef was untested.

He went below to stow gear and prepare the cabin. Jazmyn lay sprawled on the bunk where he had placed her last night, her thin shirt undulating in the breeze generated by the small fan he had pointed at her. The combination of alcohol and NyQuil had done the trick—and then some. She was still snoring when he touched her shoulder.

Ideally, he would have woken her, said goodbye, and set her on the dock, but she was going nowhere, and he didn't want to waste any time. It was going to be a six to eight-hour trip, and if he left now, he could be back by dark. She rolled over, exposing her butt to him in rebuttal as he worked around her, preparing the cabin.

Expecting at least four-foot seas, he stowed all the loose objects, checked the cabinet latches, and made sure the hatches were all closed and locked. With the GPS in hand, he went back on deck and started the GPS unit leaving it to acquire the satellites and position while he prepared the dock lines. One at a time he looped each line around the dock cleat and brought the end back to the cockpit, instead of having them tied off on the cleat. It took several minutes he didn't want to waste, but with the wind pushing the boat into the side of the dock, he would need to release the lines in sequence to get away with no damage.

A quick glance assured him that everything was ready, and an inspection of the gas tank revealed a little over half a tank. He squeezed the priming bulb, opened the tank vent, and pulled the choke out. It took half a dozen pulls before the engine coughed, and then several more before it started. With the choke pushed in, the small outboard started to even out.

He looked up at the sky and saw the moon a few inches above the horizon, Venus a dull glow beside it. That should give him enough light to navigate the intracoastal and Pass-A-Grille channel. Once he reached open water, he would be fine in the hour of darkness that would remain before sunrise. He released the bow and stern lines and pulled them into the boat. The only thing stopping the hull from colliding with the dock now was the aft spring line. Reaching back, he set the engine in reverse and released it. Quickly, he turned the throttle and the boat slid backward, away from the dock.

Once into the waterway, he lashed the tiller and stowed the

lines and fenders. The moonlight lit the channel, clearly illuminating the markers as the boat coasted by them. A half-hour later, he was past the last lighted buoy and into open water. He lashed the tiller again, loosened the main sheet and raised the halyard. The wind coming from dead ahead allowed him to raise the mainsail without stopping or changing course. The sail flapped in the breeze as he placed the halyard onto the winch and cranked until the luff of the sail was tight against the mast.

Back at the tiller, he steered twenty-five degrees off the wind and watched as the sail filled. With his course established and the wind powering the boat, he shut down the engine. It was always exhilarating when the only noise was the sound of the boat as it slid through the water, but the sensation was dulled this morning with Kyle gone and the girl below. Next, he released the furling line and pulled out the jib. The speed picked up noticeably as the genoa unfurled. A glance at the GPS revealed that he was making nine knots.

He adjusted the course to the bearing shown on the screen and watched the speed rise to 9.5 knots as the boat settled into a beam reach. If he could maintain this speed, he would reach the cluster of waypoints by early afternoon. Hopefully Kyle would still be alive.

* * *

Dick woke on a couch — one that he had never slept on before, and he had slept on plenty. He sat up and looked around the room, trying to piece together where he was. Things weren't that bad, he figured, as it took seconds rather than minutes to realize he was at Sheryl's. She had nagged him to stay over after a round of smoking and drinking when they got back to her place late last night or early in the morning, depending how you looked at it.

He didn't need much persuasion — her weed was good.

Taking the room in, he walked over to a bookcase and

noticed several pictures of her holding some large tarpon and bonefish, then went to the tray left from last night on the bar by the kitchen. Breaking apart several buds, he rolled a joint and lit it.

"Pretty early for that," Sheryl said as she came out of the bedroom, dressed in workout clothes.

He held the smoke in for a second before releasing it and answering, "Never too early. This is good. Didn't know you fished." He pointed to the pictures.

"That was with Will." She stopped in mid-sentence. "I'm going for a run. Be back in forty-five minutes. I'll make something to eat when I get back, if you're still going to be here."

He looked around and took another hit. "Yeah. Can I use your phone? I want to see if I can find out anything about Kyle."

She nodded and left. He hadn't wanted to mention Will's name in front of her. Every time he had brought it up, she became morose. He took another hit from the joint and pulled his wallet from his pocket. On the back of a tattered business card, he found Will's number, and went to the landline on the table.

No one answered, though, and he hung up, realizing it might have been the caller ID that had stopped Will from answering. He would have to find another phone to contact him. Without much hope, he picked up the phone again and dialed Kyle's cell phone. It went immediately to voicemail. He hung up and looked at the pile of buds on the tray, trying to figure out if he could liberate a few joints worth to get him through the day.

Hungry, he went to the refrigerator and scoured the contents, emerging with eggs, ham, cheese, and some vegetables. He had onion sautéing in butter when she walked back in.

"Hey. Figured I'd just make something. Hope that's okay," he said.

She looked at the pan and ingredients and nodded. "It wasn't going to be as good if I cooked. I'm going to shower, and then we're going to figure out what to do about Kyle."

Dick snapped back to reality. "Okay, yeah." He finished the omelet and set out two plates. She emerged from the bedroom in a robe, with a towel slung around her hair. He looked at her, wondering how Will could let her get away. Most of the girls he knew were of the meaner, self-serving variety. But she seemed sincere and just nice.

Then again, he'd seen it all. Not the best-looking guy, and usually too stoned to be a threat, he had plenty of girls that poured out their hearts to him. He decided to try and get her talking and see what she was all about.

She dug into the breakfast, rebuffing his attempts at conversation. When she finished eating, she turned to him and the questions started. He looked at the tray, hoping she would offer another joint to get him through the interrogation.

She must have seen him staring at the tray. "Come on, Dick. You can have some when you answer."

He started to fidget in the chair as he gave her a recount of the last few days. The look in her eyes grew more serious as the story unfolded, her concern evident when Will's name was mentioned.

"Holy crap, you guys are in this much trouble and not one of you thought to call the police?"

She reached for the phone, but he stopped her. "They'll put me in jail for my warrants for sure, and probably take Will with me for being an accomplice. There's no evidence left, and just our word that Kyle was taken. This isn't going to play out well."

She thought for a few minutes. "Will introduced me to the guy that owns the fish house. He's at least indirectly involved in this, anyway. Maybe he can help."

Anything was better than the police. "Okay. Just no cops."

* * *

Will estimated they were twenty miles off the coast when the sun emerged from the clouds. The wind had picked up noticeably, and he had reefed the mainsail. The only problem was the seas; the bigger swells were five feet now, and they threw spray over the bow all the way to the cockpit as the boat surged through them. If they got any bigger, he would have to furl the jib and lose even more speed.

He had almost forgotten about the girl when she emerged from the cabin. With a look of disgust cast his way, she went to the leeward bench, which was closer to the water, with the boat heeled over, and leaned over the side. He could tell she was in a bad way as her back convulsed with each heave. She stayed there for a long minute before she turned and wiped her mouth on her blouse.

"What the fuck did you give me, and where are we? You didn't say anything about a fucking sail." The rant continued for a minute before she took a breath, went back to the gunwale, and leaned over again.

There was nothing like watching a girl throw up to put you off her, but he didn't turn away, as she emptied what was left in her stomach. Without a word, she turned and glared at him before stumbling down the steps to the cabin and disappearing. He almost laughed to himself about the difference a night and some weather could make. Last night, he couldn't take his eyes off her; today he didn't want to look.

And then his thoughts turned to Sheryl. Maybe it had taken last night to appreciate her. He lashed the tiller and went into the cabin, casting a quick look at the bundle of misery curled up on the bench, thankfully facing away from him. That was the price he would have to endure for his infatuation.

Quickly grabbing the cell phone from the chart table, hoping she wouldn't turn and confront him again, he went back on deck.

He stared at the phone, feeling a connection as the screen showed Sheryl's number as a missed call. Reluctant, or maybe plain scared to call back, he stared at the phone, hoping it would ring and be her to break the ice. Better if she called first. A large wave jarred the boat, breaking him from his thoughts.

A glance over the rail and he estimated the seas had risen another foot since he had last checked. The GPS showed they were making almost ten knots now. Just thirty miles from the group of waypoints; well past the halfway mark, he thought as he adjusted the sails and reviewed his options. The weather had called for fifteen to twenty-knot winds, and from the look of it, they were over that now.

Hoping for the best, and with only a few hours to sail before he reached his destination, he decided to hold course.

* * *

"What do you mean you lost the fish?" the voice yelled.

The boat was rocking on its anchor in a hundred twenty feet of water. "We got one in the box already, and I'm planning to stay out until we get another. Just settle down," Greg screamed into the phone over the wind.

"You fool. The one in the cooler. There are at least three people that know about it now. What are you going to do about them?"

Greg looked over at Kyle. "I've got one handled. I'll deal with the other two when I get back in. I know where to find them."

"This isn't good. Maybe you should come back in now."

Greg looked at the seas. They had built over the last few hours, but the NOAA report said this was the peak. Although it was uncomfortable to be anchored and fishing in these conditions, he knew from experience that you got the biggest fish in the biggest seas. He would wait it out and run back when the wind calmed.

"Give me a few more hours."

"I'll cut you out of this deal so quick--" The voice was halted by the scream of the clicker. He turned and saw line pouring off the reel.

"Big fish, gotta go." Greg ended the call and went for the anchor ball. One of the deckhands had instantly gone for the rod and was working it furiously. Greg watched him as he clipped the hook on the anchor line and released it from the cleat. From the looks of it, the fish was big enough they would have to chase it and retrieve the anchor later. He went to the helm and started the engine, turning around to see which way the fishing line was going out before pushing the two levers to forward. Turning to port, he swung the boat in a wide circle, keeping an eye on both the line and the deckhand frantically reeling in the slack as he closed on the fish. This kind of fishing was all about teamwork, not individual glory. It mattered that they brought back fish, not who reeled it in.

The fish must have sensed the boat as it closed, and it started to peel off line at a furious pace. It crossed behind the boat, and Greg had to abandon the wheel and help the angler switch the rod to the holder on the other side. They had to keep the line away from the propellers at all costs. Just as they were about to set the rod in the holder, the fish reversed again and they struggled to take the rod back to the original position when one engine suddenly stalled.

"It's in the prop. We're screwed!" Greg yelled as he furiously tugged on the line. He felt the tension ease as the friction of the line against both itself and the steel of the propeller weakened the monofilament. Then it parted and the fish was gone.

Chapter 14

Sheryl could hear the yelling from the waiting area. Maybe it was just business, but there was no mistaking Lance's voice. She had never seen this side of him. Wondering, she wrinkled her nose from the smell of fish permeating the air-conditioned office, looking at the secretary who appeared not to notice.

The facility was located in an older section of St. Petersburg, next to the railroad tracks. Through a plate glass window, she could see the fish processing and warehouse facility filled with stainless steel sinks and tables and giant walk-in coolers and freezers. She sat next to Dick, who was fidgeting in the old vinyl chair. His constant anxiety was starting to wear on her. They had gone by the fish house first, to see if Will knew anything, but he was gone. The building was locked up. His truck was there, the boat was not, lowering him another notch in her eyes. He should be working. And to think, she had been kind of excited to see him.

Lance was the only other person she knew that had any ties to this. He owned the building and the cooler where everything seemed to be happening, and although Dick had said that he leased it to some guy named Greg, he was still the logical place to start. Maybe he had contacts with the Department of Fish and Game, or knew someone else that could help without running Dick's name through the computer and landing him in jail.

The office was quiet now, the phone call over, and a minute later, Lance emerged from the office and came toward them. She stood to shake his hand, kicking Dick in the leg to do the same.

"Hi, Sheryl," he said.

She smiled back. They had met several times. "And this is Dick. He was working for Will on the project." She noticed his brow furrow.

"Good to meet you." He placed a hand on Dick's back to lead them into his office. She watched him as he squirmed under the man's touch, wondering who had raised him to be such a mess.

They took the two chairs on the visitor's side of the desk while Lance went around to the business side and sat. She looked around the office, unable to avoid noticing the civic awards mounted on every wall. Pictures of Little League teams and Girl Scout troops covered every surface.

"I don't want to trouble you with this, but seeing that it's your building, you're kind of involved, anyway."

His gaze moved to Dick and his brow furrowed again. She realized that he might be thinking this was some kind of worker complaint, and started right in on their story to diffuse his concern. He relaxed as she spoke, then sat upright at the mention of the tuna and Kyle's abduction.

"Now wait a minute. Just because I own the property, don't think I have any involvement in this," he cut her off.

"No. No. No," she stammered, not wanting him on the defensive. "I just thought since you knew the area and Greg, that you might be able to point us in the right direction.

"And you don't want to go to the police?"

Dick shook his head violently and started to tremble.

"No, there's too much that would be misconstrued and it would probably shut the job down as a crime scene. They might try and arrest Will. What about Fish and Game?"

He leaned back. "I could make a call, but they're so undermanned I don't know what they would do. I hear you about the police. This is messy. If we can just get the boy back without trouble, I can handle Greg. I can look the other way about the black market fish if he moves off my property."

She was glad he saw it in such simple terms. Stopping the poaching was high on her list, right after getting Kyle back, but she knew better than to push too hard. Dick seemed to be better as well. He was still fidgeting, but the red color on his neck that had been building through the conversation was a light pink, now, and fading.

Lance picked his cell phone up off the desk, scrolled through a few screens, and put it to his ear. A minute later, someone must have answered, and she listened to the one-sided conversation.

"You still out there?" he asked.

She could hear what sounded like muffled yelling on the other end, but could not make out the words.

Lance held the phone away from his ear as the voice continued. Finally he asked, "Who's with you?" He waited for the answer. "Give me your coordinates." He wrote some numbers on a pad and hung up.

"So what should we do?" she asked as he sat there staring at the phone. The call had clearly upset him, but he wasn't sharing details.

"Give me a minute and let me think this out." He leaned back. "Where's Will?

She looked at Dick, who was rocking in the chair. He looked better than before, but better for him was relative. They would have to get out of here soon, before he lost control. "He took that stupid boat he bought out for a sail. He'd have to have a reason to skip work and do that." She realized that she was defending him.

Lance looked at her harshly. "You mean he's not working?"

"That's right. His truck's at the fish house, but the boat is gone," she said, wondering why he seemed more upset about the job than Kyle. "We need to do something."

"You're right. Why don't we take a ride to the beach, try and find Greg. Maybe Will'll be back by then. If they're both gone, I have a good idea where Greg might be."

She was grateful enough for someone to take charge that she didn't question him. Dick was already on his feet when Lance rose and went to the door. They followed him into the waiting area.

"Hold on. I'll be right back." He turned and went back to the office.

They stood waiting and after a moment he returned, jingling his keys as if he had forgotten them.

* * *

Spindrift was streaming perpendicular to the white-capped waves now—a sure sign the wind had picked up to twenty-five knots. Not that he needed a reference. He had added another reef to the main sail and furled the jib to a third of its normal size. The boat maintained course, although he needed to constantly adjust the main sheet to compensate for the weather helm pulling the boat hard to windward with each gust.

They were making headway, but as he glanced at the GPS he saw that their speed was down to five knots. The lack of sail area and heavy seas breaking over the bow slowed their progress.

The girl had stuck her head out of the cabin an hour ago, given him a disgusted look, and gone back to bed. Now he could see movement below, and waited for her inevitable appearance.

"You should drink some water," he called into the cabin. "You're probably dehydrated."

"Why? So you can watch me puke my guts out some more? Are you the kind of guy that enjoys this?" She came onto deck and sat across from him. These were the first words she had spoken in hours. "Turn us around and go back. I will make it worth your while."

The thought of touching her repulsed him, now. He had realized hours ago that he had made a huge mistake breaking up with Sheryl. "Relax. We're almost there."

"Where?" She looked around. "The middle of fucking nowhere. Zadrota." Her accent was harsh when she cursed. She leaned back against the gunwale and swallowed hard, then quickly turned and stuck her head over the side.

"Please, drink some water. You really will feel better." He tried to soothe her as she turned back around, but her blue eyes pierced his flesh as she glared at him. Then she got up to go back to the cabin, but just as she took her first step, a large wave caught the boat. The hull turned toward the wind and rolled in the trough. The girl was caught on her feet and quickly lost balance, skidding across the deck to the leeward bench. Will was too slow in correcting the boat and it spun, causing her momentum to increase.

Her ankle caught the jib sheet and she was over the side.

He had no control of the boat now. The sequence of events had happened too quickly for him to react. The PFD on the rail was already in the water, thrown as soon as he saw her go over, its line trailing behind it. He was standing trying to spot her, but with white caps breaking everywhere, it was impossible to see her. To make matters worse, the wind was blowing in the same direction of where he suspected she was, moving her away from the boat and making it impossible to hear her if she screamed.

The PFD was visible, and he had to assume it was drifting in the same direction as the girl. Just as he thought it, he spotted a head bobbing in the waves. The split second loss of concentration had caused a jibe and the boom swung hard across as the boat, nailing him in the head. He went to his knees.

His head throbbed as he lay on the deck, the sail flapping in the wind above him. The boom was swinging back and forth, causing the canvas and lines to slam against each other and the rigging, disorienting him as much as the injury. Not sure if he had lost consciousness or not, he remembered the girl, and struggled to his feet, staying low to avoid the boom. He scanned the water, but there was nothing in sight; not the PFD or the blond head. Terrified at what had happened, he struggled into the cabin to call the Coast Guard.

As his foot hit the first step, another wave lifted the bow and pitchpoled the boat into the trough. Already unsteady on his feet from the boom, he slammed into the cabin head-first and fell to the deck.

* * *

Greg leaned over the transom and cut the line, grabbing the end before it was lost in the waves. The fouled engine was raised and almost horizontal to the seas, the blade of the propellor dipping into the water every time the boat bounced. Slowly, he tried to work the cut line backward around the shaft, but he didn't have the reach. Someone was going to have to get wet.

He stood up and looked at his choices. The crewman was not the brightest bulb in the ceiling. He could do it, but why risk injury? Plus, Greg needed his help to fish. It was almost impossible to single hand a large bluefin.

The boy caught his attention. "You. Come over here. Maybe you'll be useful after all." He waited as the kid named Kyle approached. "What you need to do is climb over the transom and hug that engine. Once you're out there, you can untangle the line. Piece of cake."

Kyle was clearly unsure.

"Here, I'll tie a line around you just in case." Greg opened a hatch and pulled out a coiled dock line, which he tossed to Kyle. "Put it around your waist."

Kyle was in the water a minute later, riding the outboard motor like a bucking bronco. Slowly, he seemed to get in sync with the seas, and started to work the monofilament off the propeller.

"Good work. Let me help you." Greg grabbed the line and pulled. He caught Kyle off balance, but the boy recovered and was back over the transom.

Greg ignored the trembling figure in front of him. Soaking wet, the wind chilling him, Kyle went and huddled under the protection of the small console. With the engine back in the water, Greg bumped the throttle into forward gently confirming that the propeller was functional. He pushed down harder on the throttle, and the boat started to move.

He steered a wide circle and the boat came around a hundred eighty degrees, on a course toward land.

"Enough for this trip." He turned to the deck hand. "This wind is crazy shit, and not going anywhere. Un-fishable, if you ask me. Screw that guy. What's he going to do if we don't bring in two? I'd rather make the run back in the daylight with these conditions."

"What about him?" The man was looking at Kyle.

"Was going to dump him, but losing the fish gave me an idea." He pushed the throttle near its limit and the boat launched over the waves, surfing the crests and struggling in the troughs.

Chapter 15

Sheryl felt strange as they pulled into the parking lot of the fish house in Kyle's car. It felt as if she didn't belong here after breaking up with Will, and she wondered how the wheel of fate had brought her back here and what it meant. Will's truck sat unmoved from this morning, and a quick glance around the corner of the building revealed that the boat was still gone.

She opened the door and got out, thankful for the fresh air. The windows had been rolled down on the drive over, but between the smell of pot and fish slime on the backseat, she was queasy. Dick had lit a joint as soon as they left Lance's office. Her first reaction was to ask him not to, but he seemed to calm down as soon as he inhaled. Maybe it was better than a half dozen pills, if that's what worked for him. Ending the medicinal marijuana debate in her head, she looked back toward the road, waiting for Lance's SUV to pull in.

She had a bad feeling about what was transpiring. Will leaving work was not all that surprising — if he were fishing. But shutting down the only job he had and going out for a sail was not like him. She had to admit she was worried, and deep down missed him. But the loss of Kyle was what was driving her. The boys had struck a chord with her, it was hard not to like them. There was also something about Lance that was bothering her, but she was having trouble focusing, and couldn't pin it down.

"Got any more of that?" she asked Dick. He gave her one of his queer looks, like it was okay for him, but not for her. "It *is* mine, remember. I know you took some off the tray." She hoped it would settle her nerves.

He looked down, hesitated, and then reached into his pocket for the half smoked joint. "Here. I could use a little more, too."

She took the joint back to the car and waited for him. They each rolled up their windows and he lit up. Soon she felt much better. Maybe he was onto something. Then a glint of metal flashing in the sun caught her eye. She looked back and saw the SUV pull in the lot. She quickly exited the car hoping a cloud of smoke didn't follow her.

Dick stayed, the yellow glow of the joint in his mouth. Rather than have Lance come to the car and see what they were doing, she went to him.

"Where's your boat?"

"They should have it in the water now." He looked over at the large metal building filled with racks holding boats of all sizes. A forklift was moving forward into one of the bays. It grabbed the underside of a hull, reversed, and navigated toward the ramp. The driver lowered the forks and the boat dropped into the water.

"There we go." Lance moved toward the boat.

She glanced behind her at the car and waved for Dick to get out and follow. Together, they walked toward the boat, where Lance stood at the helm with the motor running.

"Come 'on aboard," he yelled over the engine's rumble.

Sheryl hopped into the boat, admiring the luxurious fittings. It was certainly not a fishing boat. About thirty feet long, shaped slightly beamier than a cigarette boat, it was all leather and stainless steel. And spotless. She had never seen a boat gleam like this. Looking down at her feet, she realized that she was leaving a trail of dirt behind her.

"Don't worry about that. Get settled and we can get out of here."

She looked at Dick, who was looking warily at the boat. By now she knew his ticks, and one was definitely coming on. Having him along might be more of a liability than a help if he started getting anxious, or worse.

"Why don't you stay here and keep an eye out? If Greg or Will show up, you can give us a call."

He looked relieved. "Okay, but I got no phone. Kyle has ours."

She thought for a second and tossed him hers. "Be careful with it." Then she turned to Lance. "Can you text him your number so he can call us if anything happens here?"

Lance handed her his phone, she entered the number and sent it to her phone. "You know how to use that, right?"

Dick gave her one of his looks. "What do you think? I'm not from the olden days."

Satisfied that she had made the right decision, she settled into the soft caress of the seat and waited for Lance to pull away. He went to the bow and released the dock line, then came back to the helm and backed toward open water. When they reached the end of the pier, he turned and straightened the boat before putting it into forward and pushing down on the throttle.

The air felt good on her face as the boat picked up speed, and she watched the white sand beach of Shell Key disappear in the distance. Used to the ride of Will's flats boat, where you felt the water, she noticed that the heavier boat cut through the waves, parting them with huge swaths of white spray. Despite the circumstances, she found herself enjoying the ride. The engines were too loud for conversation, which suited her. Lance was busy working some kind of computer screen set into the dashboard. She looked over to try and see what he was doing, and saw a chart of the area with a line they were following leading to a cross. That must be their destination.

The novelty of the ride quickly wore off and she returned to the thought that she couldn't pin down earlier. How did he know where to go? The Gulf was huge, with no landmarks like the Keys. There, if you told someone you were going out by Sombrero Light on the reef, they knew where you would be. Here, once you were out of sight of land, it was just open water.

Suddenly the speed dropped as he eased off the throttles and pulled the phone from his pocket. It must have been on vibrate, she thought, as there was no way he could hear it ring over the engines. Even at idle speed the engine was too loud for her to hear any of the conversation.

But something must have happened, because he swung the wheel and turned the boat back toward shore.

* * *

Will thought he heard a scream and something slam against the hull, but his ears were ringing from the blows to his head, and he couldn't be sure. Slowly he rose from the deck, careful that he didn't follow the girl overboard. Finally, he was able to pull his body high enough to see over the gunwale. He pulled on the jib sheet, which was hanging over the side, but felt resistance. With both hands, he hauled and the line started to move.

On his knees, he peered over the side and saw her body caught in the line. Her head was bobbing in the water, submerged each time the boat hit a trough. Will gathered his strength and started to haul her back onto the boat. When her body reached the side, though, he lost his leverage and was unable to pull anymore. He dragged the line to the winch, used to trim the sails, took three loops around the cylinder, and started to pull. The mechanical advantage helped, but he had to resort to the winch handle for the final few feet. She came aboard an inch at a time.

The effort was monstrous, his head still spinning from the effects of the boom hitting him. Once she was aboard, he sat back, trying to catch his breath, and unable to even assess her situation for several minutes. Finally he was able to get his head straight, and went to her. She was conscious, but appeared out of it. Probably a good thing, as he anticipated the tongue lashing he was destined for when she came to. He sat her up on the cockpit floor, using the benches on either side to keep her from falling over, and started to organize the boat.

First he released the tension from the sheets, allowing the sails to flag. Then he sorted out the lines, pulling the jib sheet that had taken her overboard back onto the boat. As soon as the lines were organized, he tightened the main sheet and set course back to the marina. Considering the weather and what had just happened, it was the only move he had.

The ride was slower but more comfortable with the wind and seas behind them. The boat no longer fought him, and settled into the rhythm of the waves, allowing the wind to push it forward. He lashed the tiller and went to the cabin, where he grabbed a bottle of water and drank deeply. Back on deck, he went to the girl and placed his hands against her face. Devoid of makeup and her hair a wet mop, she barely resembled the girl he had fallen for last night.

She seemed to respond to his touch, and suddenly reached up and grabbed his hand. Her eyes cracked open, and she shrieked. Before he could calm her, she head-butted him in the forehead. He staggered backward and sat facing her.

"I'm sorry. We're headed back," he said, trying to diffuse her anger. "I'll drop you wherever you want."

She grabbed the bottle of water from his hand. "Yes, you will. I want money too. Ten thousand dollars you owe me, or I will go to the police. And if you don't pay me, I will send Gregori to help me collect."

He didn't doubt her threat, and added the debt to the running total in his mind that the few dollars in his pocket would not cover. He thought about Kyle and hoped he was still alive, but at this point his mission was over. He'd get back, dump the girl, call the police, and get back to work — probably what he should have done in the first place.

He adjusted their course slightly to the south and trimmed the sails. The high rises on St. Pete Beach had come into view, the pink stucco and white turrets of the Don Cesar hotel a clear landmark. For the first time since the girl had walked into the bar last night, he felt like he was thinking with his own brain.

Half an hour later, the first green marker slid by the port side of the boat and the seas started to subside. Another hundred yards and they were in flat water for the first time in eight hours. He started the engine and turned the boat into the wind to take the sails down. After furling the jib, he released the main sheet and went to drop the halyard, when a boat cruised past, going far faster than the no-wake signs called for.

He rose to see who it was, but the sail blocked his view and he was thrown off balance as the wake hit the hull. Back at the winch, he tensioned the halyard and released the one-way block. The sail dropped quickly and he turned north into the intracoastal waterway, heading toward the marina.

Jazmyn glared at him from across the cockpit. She had one of his shirts on, the tails barely covering her legs. Usually that look worked for him, but her luster had long worn off. He tried to ignore her as he turned left and entered the dock area.

"Take me to Gregori's," she ordered.

Without a word, he pushed the tiller and swung the boat back into the main channel. It would be far better to drop her there than to disembark at the marina and have to drive her somewhere. He had no desire to be seen with her.

There was little traffic on the intracoastal today, the wind and seas keeping the fair weather boaters home. With no help from the girl, even if she actually knew how to find the house from the water, he made two wrong turns, but soon found the house. Greg's boat was tied up at the dock and Will tensed, ready for a confrontation, but there was no one in sight as he eased the boat in.

She was ready, bag in hand when the hull touched the dock, and easily jumped the one foot space.

Before she turned to leave, she looked at him. "Ten thousand dollars. I will not forget."

He turned away from her, reached around the outboard engine, and slammed the boat in reverse, wanting to get out of there before Greg saw him. Any confrontation right now would end badly. Injured and without any kind of weapon, he stood no chance against the larger man. The lump on his forehead from where the boom had struck him was throbbing, and Kyle weighed heavily on his mind as he motored back to the marina. It was time for the police.

Chapter 16

Back at the marina, Will tied the boat off and sat down. His head was still pounding, his vision slightly blurred, plus he had a slight metallic taste in his mouth that he couldn't pinpoint the cause of. But the relief at getting the girl off the boat almost put a smile on his face. As rose slowly and stepped onto the dock, wavering slightly. Not sure if it was the effects of the boom striking him, the head-butt, or just being in big seas all day, he struggled down the dock toward the parking lot, realizing that one of the symptoms of a concussion was not remembering the symptoms.

Not that it mattered. Kyle's car was still parked there, reminding him of his failure. He did a double take, looking at the car again. The windows were fogged up, a cloud of smoke filling the interior.

Dick jumped when he knocked on the window. He cracked it and Will stepped back as the smoke started to escape. Dick was visible now, a smile on his face. "'Sup, dude?"

"What the hell are you doing sitting out here smoking? How is this going to help Kyle?" Will vented.

"Easy, man. What am I supposed to do? You're not here and Sheryl took off with that Lance dude. You know that creep that owns the place. She gave me her phone and told me to hang out and wait for you. So I'm hanging out." He got out of the car.

Will stood back to get away from the smoke; surely that couldn't be good for his head. "Maybe you'd better fill me in on a few things. How did Lance get involved, and why is she with him?" He reached for the phone in Dick's hand, thinking he might get a better answer from her directly.

"Call Lance's phone," Dick said.

Will scrolled through the contacts, found the number, and hit dial. He paced back and forth, waiting for an answer, but after half a dozen rings, the call went to voicemail. Frustrated, he left a quick message to call him back and pressed end.

"No one answered," he said as he returned to the car where Dick was leaning against the hood. "Let's have it—the whole story, from when I left you on the boat."

He listened as Dick went through what had happened since Will left for the bar the night before. He didn't trust Dick to remember everything, especially in this state, but at least he had an idea of what was going on now.

He went to the curb in front of the building and sat down, realizing for the first time all day how hungry and tired he was. Sheryl's phone was in his hand and he checked the time. Almost five. Too late to get any work done, not that he felt up to it. He stood up, reached into his pocket, and pulled out the wet bills. It wasn't going to get him far, but he needed some food.

"Hey. You hungry?" he asked Dick. Maybe some food would help his head.

Dick looked up suspiciously. "Who, me?"

"Yeah. I got enough for a couple of burgers if you want to run and get them. I'll stay here and wait for Lance and Sheryl to come back."

"You don't have to ask twice," Dick said as he went toward Will and grabbed the money from his hand. He went back to the car, started it up, and pulled out of the lot.

Will stuffed the last damp bill in his pocket. He was fraught with guilt about Kyle, but decided to put off the decision about what to do until Lance called back, and they could decide whether to involve the police. He was either dead or not, and in his present condition there was not much he could do about it. For now, he had to focus on the job, or he was going to be flat broke.

He got up, opened the lock on the door, and walked through the building, trying to make mental notes of what needed to be done next, but he was too distracted to think straight. Between his head throbbing and the uncertainty about Kyle, all he wanted to do was to sit down and wait for someone to call with the answer. But he knew the best course was to try and stay busy. That would at least keep Lance happy and put some money in his pocket.

Most of the work was underneath, and he would need help for that. With Kyle gone, Dick was all he had left. It was going to be hard, but he had little choice. He left the building and went to the seawall. The platform was still tied up. Slowly, he sat down and slid on, rather than chance a fall, then freed the line. He got to his feet and moved the raft under the building.

The raft rocked from the wake of a boat and he looked out. A large cruiser was pulling into the space between the fish house and marina. It coasted to the dock used by the fork lift to dry dock the boats. The engine cut off and he could hear voices. One of them sounded like Sheryl, and he pulled himself toward that side of the building to hear the conversation.

He stopped five feet from the edge, hopefully invisible to the people in the boat.

"What do we do now?" he heard Sheryl ask.

"See if he's here, I guess. I think that's the boat he bought. It was the only sailboat here for sale, and the sign's gone."

It was Lance. Relieved that they were back, and hoping for some guidance, he started to pull himself out of the building when he heard Kyle's car pull up.

117

Will summoned his courage and pulled himself into the open at the same time as Dick came around the corner, munching on a fry with a bag of food in his hand.

"What's going on Will?" Lance snapped as he emerged into daylight.

Lance turned to him, allowing Sheryl time to jump onto the dock.

"Just checking things out for tomorrow," he said.

"Where the hell have you been all day? I've lost a day's work and had to deal with her all day, looking for you and your boy, who stuck his head where it didn't belong."

Will stuttered, "I was trying to find him."

"Well? From the look of you, it didn't go too well."

"No luck. I know Greg has him, but I guess you know that too. I headed out to try and find him, but had to turn back."

"It's a pretty big ocean out there, if you don't know where to look. You need to be on this job. Don't make me regret my decision to hire you. There are plenty of guys with licenses and insurance I could have used. But I took a chance on you, and you're letting me down."

Will was speechless. He knew Lance had tried to get bids from licensed contractors, but most wouldn't even look at the job. The ones that would were almost four times the cost he had estimated. This was a side of Lance that he hadn't seen, and he decided to keep Greg's GPS to himself.

"We'll be back on the job tomorrow." He looked at Dick for confirmation, but he was sitting on the curb, knuckles deep in a burger, oblivious to the conversation. "And what's with you two?"

Sheryl looked at Lance. "Nothing." She moved over by Dick.

Lance hopped off the boat to let the forklift hoist it from the water, spoke to the driver, and then turned to Will. "Tomorrow, you be on the job. I have some resources that I can get to find the boy. I'll take care of that, just get this thing done." He turned and walked toward his SUV.

"What's up with all that?" he asked Sheryl.

"Good to see you, too. Think we can talk somewhere?" she asked. "You look bad."

It almost sounded as if she cared. "I've got to eat. You hungry?"

"As a matter of fact, yes."

Will took the bag from Dick and started walking toward the boat. "You coming?"

"Sure, the scene of the crime. I might as well see where our future went." She looked toward the parking lot at the empty space where Lance's SUV had been and then followed him down the dock.

He offered a hand to help her aboard, but she declined and jumped onto the deck.

"You want to tell me your side of this mess? I got Dick's, but I want to hear it from you." She sat on the same bench that Jazmyn had sat on the night before.

Will looked at her and started to wonder about the karma of the boat. "Sure." He opened the bag and offered her the burger and fries. Suddenly, he was not hungry. While she ate, he recounted the story from where Dick had first discovered the fish. She nodded several times, as if confirming to herself that he was telling the truth. There was no reason to mention the girl and muddy the waters, so he left her out, but told everything else.

"What's the deal with Lance?" he asked.

"That guy creeps me out. I know you think he's helping you out, but I think you're saving his ass. I overheard a couple of suspicious conversations."

Will searched his memory for anything Lance had said or done that was suspicious, but came up with nothing. He had been pushy, but most bosses were. Wondering if she was exaggerating, he decided to let it go. "What kind of threats was he making?"

"Not anything overt. Just that I should keep you focused on the job and not let you get involved with Greg. I don't think he's the guy you think he is. When Dick and I were in his office, he was yelling at some guy about fishing or something. It's really suspicious that he has a processing plant, this fish house and the cooler; that's a lot of coincidences. I'm pretty sure he's in some kind of financial trouble, too. There were some papers on his desk from a bank."

"I don't know. He's always been good to me."

"As long as you do what he wants. And he needs you to finish the building. I'm telling you, there's more here than meets the eye."

Will looked at her. "Why don't you stay here if it makes you feel any better?" Afraid of rejection he added, "But if you want to go, you can take the truck."

"Thanks. Maybe I will stay, but just tonight. I'm pretty strung out from this. At least I'll know where you are. From the look of your head, somebody needs to keep an eye on you." She gave him the first kind look since she had sat down.

"Let me go talk to Dick about tomorrow. There's a wine cooler in the fridge if you want it." He got up and stepped off the boat, wanting to look back at her, but deciding not to push his luck. They had been together long enough that he knew if he gave her some space, she would come around.

Dick was still sitting on the curb when he approached. "Work tomorrow?"

"Yeah, I guess. What about Kyle?"

"Lance said he had some connections and would take care of it. I suspect he will." If Lance was mixed up in this, making some progress on the building might just make Kyle reappear.

"I'm going to need to get paid soon."

Will nodded. "We get some work done then I can get another

draw. Won't be more than a couple of days."

Dick got up and went to the car. It started and he pulled out. Through the open window he yelled, "Seven o'clock," and pulled away.

Will went back to the building and locked the door. He had a plan for tomorrow, and with Dick's help, they could set a couple of pilings. Enough to show Lance that he had things in hand and get some money. It was making a deal with the devil, but if it got Kyle back and some money in his pocket, he would do it. Now he had to figure out Sheryl. He fingered the wet twenty—the only thing remaining in his pocket—and decided a little wine wouldn't hurt.

* * *

"You listen to me. We need to rethink this whole thing." Lance stood in Greg's living room, fuming.

"Shit, we got it covered. We just have to stay out of the cooler until the job's done. Then we set the fish room up so when can unload from under the building, and we can crank up the operation and keep this baby running forever," Greg said.

"They know too much. Will may be a reclusive fishing guide, but the girl's pretty smart. Taking the kid was a bad move. Now it's about more than just the fish."

"They messed with our operation and I'm supposed to do nothing?" Greg asked.

"I'm telling you, they are about to connect the dots. If they put us together, we're done. I think we need to get rid of them."

"Now you're seeing things my way. I got this." Greg looked him in the eye for confirmation. "You usually stay away from this kind of stuff, so maybe you ought to get out of town for a couple of days. Let me take care of things here."

"Let him work a couple of days. We need him to finish the job. Besides being the perfect front for bringing in the fish, I need the building for my legal business. Being able to unload right from the boats as they come in will help the bottom line. With a restaurant and bar up front, that place will be a money maker."

"Whatever you say." Greg was skeptical. He didn't care much for the legal side of things.

"If we want that building finished, we need to see how he's going about it. The only other guy that was willing to work on it wanted to take the whole roof off and bring in a crane. Besides the money it would have cost, the city was going to look at that as more than fifty percent value on the building, and make us tear it down. Will is the only guy I know that can pull this off. I'm going to get some guys to help and see how he's going about it. Then he won't matter."

"Damned right. I got a guy that knows some of that construction shit, too."

Chapter 17

The heat in the v-berth was stifling, and although Will was exhausted, he had an uncomfortable night tossing and turning. Sometime during the night, he had gotten up and moved onto the deck, and now the sun woke him as it peeked above the horizon. He looked back at Sheryl, asleep on the couch, and it wasn't lost on him that Jazmyn had slept in the same place the night before.

He dismissed the women from his mind and tried to focus on the job as he climbed off the boat and looked at the building. Lance had been clear about wanting to see progress and quickly. He pulled out his phone and checked the time. With half an hour before he was suppose to be there, he knew, counting on Dick showing up on time was delusional. Maybe having his best friends life in the balance would change things. He needed help, but with the single bill left in his pocket it was going to be hard to find anyone, leaving Dick his only option.

He walked across the street and got a coffee, then walked back, opened the lock and went into the building. The two twenty-foot-long poles that he needed to set today sat on the floor. Then tomorrow, he would be able to set the beam on top of them, and a section of the floor would be done. That should be enough work to get a paycheck, and get Kyle back if Lance was true to his word. But he needed Dick to keep the schedule.

He finished the coffee, set the cup down, and got ready to prepare the poles. With a 1 1/4-inch auger bit in the drill, he set the tip to the wood and pulled the trigger. Holes needed to be bored through the top of each pole so a pipe could be slid through in order to rotate them from above and turn them into the holes while he jetted the seafloor below with a high-pressure hose. Typically, poles were set by ramming them with heavy equipment, but without removing the roof, that would be impossible.

It was slow drilling through the wet pressure-treated wood, but after a few minutes the end of the bit emerged from the other side. As he was about to start work on the second pole, he heard a car drive up. He went to the door, checking the time on his phone as he went. It was still a few minutes before seven, and he hoped no one had complained about the noise. That was all he needed. Shorthanded, he would need to work some extra hours to show Lance any progress.

He walked outside and saw a truck with two men in the front seat pull up next to his. He walked over to the driver's side and was greeted by a cigarette butt flicked from the window.

"Hey, this is private property. Can I help you guys?"

"We're supposed to show up here and ask for this guy named Will. You him?" the driver said.

"Yeah. What's this about?"

"Lance said we should come out here and help you."

Will eyed the two men. He knew he should be grateful for the help, but these guys looked like they would have a hard time walking and talking at the same time. They didn't have the sun-worn, fit look of a carpenter or even a laborer. Both were overweight, one leaning toward obese. Their greasy hair was covered with stained ball caps and their sleeveless T-shirts did little to hide their tattoos. First-class redneck wear.

"You guys got any experience?" he asked skeptically.

"Got some, but Lance said we were working, and we're here."

Will had to step back as the doors opened and the men emerged from the truck. He had little choice in the matter, but figured as long as they could do grunt work, they should be some help.

"We have to wait until seven to work around here, or the cops come. My guy should be here by then. He knows what to do up top, where you guys will be working. I'll be underneath in the water."

The man that stepped out of the passenger seat grabbed a large cooler from the back of the truck and brought it to the curb where both men sat. The lid opened and they started digging through the cavernous interior, each coming out with a large pastry.

Just as he started to drill, he heard another door slam and he went back outside, hoping it was Dick. Disappointed, but not surprised, he waited as another man exited a small truck, went to the toolbox mounted on the bed, and pulled out nail bags. He put them around his waist, reached back into the box, and pulled out a framing hammer, which he set into the loop.

Will didn't care who he was; this man was what he needed. You could usually tell a carpenter from a yahoo when they put their bags on as soon as they got to work. He glanced back at Tweedle Dee and Tweedle Dum, still sitting on the curb stuffing their faces, and shook his head.

The other man walked toward him and extended his hand. "James. Heard you need some help."

Will wasn't sure where he came from, but he looked like exactly what he needed. "Sure. Come on in and I'll show you what we're doing." He looked over at the two men on the curb. "You, too. Let's get to work."

Back inside, he finished the second hole and showed James what he had in mind. "We're going to have to rig a block and tackle from the rafters, to lift the poles through the holes. They'll still have to go through sideways, but it'll help lift them."

James looked up at the old rafters. "Gonna need to reinforce them first. You hook that load up to a single rafter and try and lift that weight, it'll bring down the roof."

Will pointed at a pile of lumber. It was nice to know there was someone that would be working up here that thought the way he did. The two rednecks were looking around the building probably for a place to nap.

"Over here, guys. Let's get these poles positioned while James hooks up the tackle." They walked over to the closest pole and stood there with their hands on their hips. "Take one of those steel pipes and slide it through the hole. Then you can drag the end here." He pointed to a spot on the floor.

James had nailed a board across several rafters and had just finished drilling a hole in the center for an eye bolt, where the block would hang from. He climbed down the ladder and stood in front of Will. "I got it up here. You gonna work the water?"

"Yeah. I'm going to jet the hole with this pump. You guys need to set the pole and rotate it. Should work." He looked James in the eye. "I'm glad you're here. Those two would probably get me killed." Will had been around construction long enough to know that hiring was often sketchy and sometimes you had to work with what walked in the door.

James gave him a big grin. Will turned away and went outside to set up the dive gear and change into his wetsuit. There was no sign of life on the sailboat as he sat on the seawall fitting the first stage of the regulator to the tank. With a wrench, he removed the air gauge and inflator hose from the first stage. He was not planning on using a BC in the ten-foot-deep water, and didn't want the gauges getting in the way. The depth was fixed and his air supply would last for hours in the shallow water. The risk of the extra gear getting hung up on something was not worth the small safety factor it supplied.

He screwed plugs into the vacant holes, turned the air on, and checked for leaks. Just as he had gotten into the three-mil wetsuit and was about to slide into the harness, he heard another car pull up.

Hoping it was Dick, he turned around, ready to give him a piece of his mind. But it was Lance, and he wished he was in the water already so that he didn't have to deal with him.

Reluctantly, he stood and walked toward him. "Morning."

"Looks like you're ready to get this done. I'm glad."

"Well, I should be thanking you for sending the help." He looked at Lance, who was watching something over his shoulder. Wondering what had distracted him, he turned and saw Sheryl walking toward them. "Hey," he called over to her.

"Hey back," she said as she approached. "Morning, Lance. Will, do you have some money so I can get some coffee and something to eat?"

Before he could answer, Lance moved toward her. "Give me a minute to have a look around, and I'll take you to breakfast."

She shrugged. "Okay. Did you call anyone about Kyle?"

"As a matter of fact, I did. A friend from Fish and Game was going to talk to the sheriff. I suspect they'll find him pretty quick." He turned to Will. "I'll keep you and the other boy out of it as long as this keeps moving along."

The threat was not lost on him. He was about to ask Sheryl not to go, but she was already moving toward the SUV. Lance was somehow mixed up in this, he just had to figure out how. But from the way it sounded, as long as he kept working, Kyle would miraculously return.

Once he had some cash and knew Kyle was safe, he could try and do something.

* * *

"You really think your friend is going to get him back?"

Sheryl asked. They sat across from each other at a restaurant overlooking the water. She felt a little Machiavellian sitting there with him. *Keep your friends close and your enemies closer*, certainly applied to this meeting.

Lance sipped his coffee. "Good chance. But never mind that. I see you stayed on Will's boat last night."

She didn't know what to think about that statement. Was he hitting on her, or just making conversation? She'd given him nothing to be jealous about. The suspicion that he was involved in this more than he let on still unsettled her, but despite his aggressive behavior yesterday, as long as they stayed in a public place, she felt safe.

"Yeah, but not like that. I had a couple glasses of wine and didn't want to drive. I don't have to work until Thursday night."

He continued to eat. Finally he put down the fork, wiped his face, and pushed the plate away. "I can give you a ride home, if you want."

She hadn't thought of that. They had used Kyle's car yesterday, and Will might need the truck. Still mad about him spending money on the sailboat and not putting it toward a car for her, she knew she had to put the anger aside and think of Kyle. If she took the truck and Will needed materials, it would slow down the job. And that might keep Lance from finding Kyle.

No matter what happened with her and Will, she wouldn't be responsible for that happening. "That would be great, if you don't mind."

"No trouble. I have a couple of stops to make on the beach before I can take you, but if you don't mind riding along, I'll drop you afterward."

"Sure. I don't have any plans."

They finished their coffee and Lance paid the check. She cringed as he put his hand on her shoulder and they walked through the door into the parking lot. Back in the SUV, he pulled out of the lot and headed north on Gulf Boulevard. Half watching where they were going and half watching the beach, she missed the street name as he turned right. After another quick turn, he pulled up in front of a house across from the water with a dock across the street. She looked over and thought the boat looked familiar.

"Want to wait here for a minute?" he said as he got out of the SUV, leaving it running so she could use the air conditioning.

She nodded and reached into her back pocket for her phone. It wasn't there, and she had to think for a few minutes before she remembered that Dick had it. Anxiety took hold of her as she realized her safety blanket was gone, and thought about bailing out of the truck and walking back to the fish house.

Her thoughts were interrupted when Lance came back out of the house. He walked to the SUV, but instead of getting in the driver's side, he went around to the passenger door and opened it. Without asking, he grabbed her arm, pulled her from the vehicle, and walked her across the street to the house.

"You could at least ask." She squirmed in his grip, but it was too tight to break away.

"Just behave, if you want the boy back unharmed."

They walked side by side into the garage and through the door to the house. He pushed her down the hallway and into the living room, where a large man sat. "This is Greg. He's going to take care of you for a little while."

"What are you talking about?" She fought his grasp.

"Well, look what we have here," Greg said as he approached, his belly reaching her before he did. "You're Will's old lady. That'll get some work out of him." He put a large hand on her shoulder and turned to Lance. "Take the boy back. At least he can help get the job done. This nice young lady will be my guest for a while."

"Did you say Will?" A girl walked into the room wearing a bathrobe, her blond hair disheveled. She sat next to Greg. "You know that idiot?"

Sheryl just stared at her, wondering where this was going.

"Bastard almost killed me in that stupid boat of his. Owes me ten grand." She turned to Greg. "You gonna take care of that for me, baby?"

He jerked his head as if he understood.

"What the hell is she talking about?" Sheryl screamed.

Chapter 18

Will was in the water when he heard an engine that sounded much closer than the other boats that had been passing by on the intracoastal waterway all morning. It wasn't loud, but from the vibration of the propeller, he knew it was close. He popped his head out of the water and saw the aluminum skiff pull up to one of the outside pilings. Seconds later, he heard a large splash, and the engine rev as it increased speed and pulled away.

It was almost noon and he had been happy with the progress his new crew had made. It was comforting having James above, supervising Tweedle Dee and Tweedle Dum, and Dick had finally showed up around an hour ago. He knew he should have been more upset with him, but he was actually grateful that he was all right. The first piling had taken several hours to set, but now that the procedure was refined, the second pile was going in quickly. If they could continue at this pace, they could start to set the beam later today.

Just as he was about to drop down again, he heard something big moving in the water nearby. He sensed it was closing in on him, and remembered the fish carcass still in the water. Suspecting a shark, he lifted himself out of the water and clung to the platform.

"Hey!" a voice yelled.

Will turned toward the sound and took off his mask. His peripheral vision restored, he saw it was a man in the water. As it moved closer, he recognized Kyle. He let loose the line tying the platform to a nearby piling, and quickly moved toward him. Kyle was exhausted, flailing in the water as Will approached. He reached for his arm and started to pull him onto the surface of the platform, but the raft shot out from under him every time he pulled.

"My feet are tied," Kyle said as he set both elbows on the plywood and caught his breath. "Just give me a minute."

Will couldn't see his feet in the murky water, but knew he wouldn't be able to haul him onboard without help. "Are you hurt?"

"No. I'm good."

"Just hold on. I'll pull us out of here," Will said as he started to pull against the floor joists. When they were out in the open, he tied the rig to the pier by the seawall and hopped into the knee-deep water. With his dive knife, he reached down and felt for the bond holding Kyle's legs together, and cut through the tie. They both walked toward the seawall and pulled themselves out of the water.

"You sure you're okay?

"Yeah. Those guys were jerks, but I'm fine. Where's Dick?"

"Dick!" Will yelled.

A few minutes later, Dick appeared. "Dude." He went to Kyle and nodded. "What the fuck happened to you?"

"Can I get out of here and get some water or something?" Kyle asked as he rose to his feet and walked toward the building.

"Sure, whatever you need." Will said as he followed him inside. Kyle went to the water jug, set his head underneath the spigot, and drank deeply. Several drafts, later he was ready to talk.

"Not much to say. We went on this boat ride and they were fishing. Caught another of those monster bluefin and then lost one.

Then they tangled the line in the prop. I swear they were going to kill me until I got the line off and they were all buddy-buddy and shit. After that they kept me in this bedroom of what looked like a real nice house. Cable TV and all."

"Did they say why they let you go?" Will asked.

"They said to tell you to keep up the good work," Kyle said. "That you would know what he meant."

"We know it was Greg. He must have had you at his house," Will said.

"Any idea what he did with the fish?" Dick jumped in.

"Nah. I think they dropped it somewhere after they dumped me off. They had a bandana covering my eyes like it was some top secret place."

"Why don't you two catch up. I'll let the guys inside know what they need to do next," Will said, and walked away.

"There's one more thing," Kyle said.

Will turned and walked back.

"I heard Sheryl's voice talking to them outside the room right before they took me out. I don't think it was a good conversation, either."

"Shit," Will said, and went inside. The three men were sitting on a pile of lumber taking a break. "You guys can take off. Come back tomorrow morning." He was too distracted to work.

* * *

"You have a plan for her?" Lance asked.

"All's I know is we better keep these two cats apart, before one of them gets scratched. I wouldn't mind seeing them go at it, though, if you know what I mean," Greg said.

"It's just leverage. Give him back the boy so he knows nothing bad's going to happen to her. If the kid's pot-soaked brain can remember the message, he'll understand," Lance said.

"Understand this. We got a run of big-ass fish going on out

there, and without the fish house for a drop-off point, it gets really dicey. I got nowhere to take them without being seen. I was starting to get worried about the cooler and then look what happens." He pointed to his head. "Greg knows," the large man said

"Just keep her here for a day or two and we can deal with Will and those boys. James is a good hand. He'll figure out how they're doing the work soon enough," Lance said.

"I'm going out again tomorrow night. I'm telling you, I haven't seen them this thick in years."

"Keep the girl here, and remember that this is bigger than a few fish. It's a long-term solution. Once that building is safe and the city is off our backs, it's perfect. The fish come in under the building out of sight and are processed before they go out the front door where the Federal Express truck is waiting to take them to Japan," Lance said.

"Yeah, I know. And a nice fish is pulling twenty large right now," Greg said.

"Let them work all day tomorrow. I'll talk to James tonight." Lance moved toward the door. "Stay with the plan. You run this off the tracks and I'll cut you out." He looked over at Sheryl and Jazmyn. "And keep those women apart."

* * *

Will went back to the sailboat after locking the building. The new guys had been upset about not getting an eight-hour day, but he promised them a full day's pay for getting so much done. He picked up the phone and scrolled to his favorites screen, where he hit Sheryl's name. The phone rang, but a male voice answered.

"Dick?"

"Dude, she gave me the phone. I forgot to give it back." He set it on the bench.

"Never mind." Will hung up and started to think. Lance's

134

involvement in this was a sure thing now. Last night, Sheryl had talked about figuring out what was going on. He had asked her not to, and now it was too much of a coincidence that she had gone to breakfast with Lance and was now at Greg's. And he'd as much as said that Kyle would be released if they got work done. Maybe the police were the best option.

He locked up the boat and walked down the dock to his truck. It started and he entered the St Petersburg police station into his map app while he waited for the air conditioning to cool the interior. A pin dropped and he hit *start*. The directions showed on the screen and he pulled out of the parking lot.

As he drove, he tried to come up with a story that wouldn't land him in trouble, but at this point the only thing that mattered was getting Sheryl back. Holding her was different than Kyle. They could scare the boy enough for him to keep quiet. Sheryl was not like that, and if they didn't know it before, they were sure to know it after spending some quality time with her.

Several minutes later, he parked and walked toward the police station. He hesitated at the door; it was his last chance to back out, but his concern about Sheryl moved him forward. The deputy at the counter looked up.

"Can I help you?"

"My girlfriend has been abducted and—"

"Slow down there, cowboy." The deputy pushed aside the paper he was reading and took out a form. "Okay. I'll ask the questions."

They went back and forth, the officer asking and Will answering.

"You mean she left willingly this morning with this guy, and you haven't seen her since. It's only five o'clock," he paused. "That's only seven hours. I can't call it a missing person until she's been gone for twenty-four hours, and even then you don't have any proof that she's really missing and not with this guy of her own accord."

"I understand that, but…" He hesitated as the man answered the phone. He was clearly on the back burner now, and unsure how deep into the story he wanted to go. The deputy seemed skeptical of him, having already filed the story in his mind as *jilted boyfriend seeks revenge.* If nothing else, the process of walking in and reporting the crime had steeled him to take action — even if he had to go it alone. It was likely that she was being held at Greg's, and he knew where he lived.

He left the station with a quick glance back at the deputy, who was deep in an obviously more important matter. It would be best to wait until dark before he went to Greg's, he thought as he started the truck and pulled onto the street. He would be too visible in daylight, and without knowing where she was being held, he would need to scout out the property.

A list formed in his mind and he started to think about a weapon.

* * *

"What are we going to do about Sheryl?" Kyle asked as they drove over the Gandy Bridge toward Tampa.

"Dude, are you freakin' crazy? You were a hostage and shit, and you still want to be involved? We still have to find some cash and pay off Rucker. You gotta know that's not coming from Will." Dick was sucking hard on the last joint he had rolled at Sheryl's. "And this is the last of our stuff."

"I know you liked her. We can't just walk away." Kyle grabbed the joint and took a hit.

Dick stared out the window. "We could just take the john boat from my dad's and be on the water in an hour. Fish 'till the tide changes and figure it out."

"I think we need to do something. We can't run away from this. What happens when the dickhead at the club finds out she's missing? She'll lose her job."

Dick continued to stare. "So you want to call the dickhead?"

"No, but I'm not just dropping this. Let's find you some weed and figure out what to do. Will owes us some money, too. It's not enough to get clear, but I don't want to let it go."

Dick turned toward him. "Fine. Just get me some stuff. This stress is killing me."

Chapter 19

Will drove north on Gulf Boulevard and turned right on Cabrillo Ave. He pulled into the large parking lot on his left, planning to walk the short distance to the house. The lot was close to empty, so he decided on a spot close to the other cars parked there, hoping to blend in. He didn't want to chance Greg driving by and noticing his truck. He locked the truck and started walking, staying to the perimeter of the lot. When he reached the street, he turned left and started to jog the quarter-mile to the house dodging the streetlights and using the darkness as cover.

The house came into sight, and he cast a glance across the street to the dock, where Greg's boat was tied up. The truck was also in the driveway, so he sprinted toward the bushes on the side. A security light came on, but he didn't hesitate, and jumped for the shrubs by the corner of the garage. Out of breath and with sweat stinging his eyes, he huddled in the bushes, trying to decide what to do. The house was lit up like a Christmas tree — too bright to even consider a look now. Resigned to wait, he rested his back against the building and slid to the ground. His surveillance mission had been reduced swatting the mosquitoes swarming around him.

Suddenly several lights went off. Growing impatient, he started to move toward a dark area when suddenly he froze, startled by the truck door slamming and the engine starting.

Glued to the spot, he waited for the truck to back out of the driveway, pivot, and watched as it headed toward Gulf Boulevard. This was his chance. Moving quickly, he crept out of the bushes and snuck around the back of the house. Unsure how long Greg would be gone, he went from window to window, peering into each as he passed. The rooms that were illuminated were empty, and it was impossible to see anything in the darkened ones.

He reached the opposite side of the house with no luck. The front was too exposed, and the rooms also appeared to have large windows—not the kind of place where he expected Sheryl would be held. The only option now was to go inside. With no sign of anyone else in the house, he crept back to see if the window he'd cracked the other night was still opened.

Carefully, he made his way back to the room. No light was visible through the blinds as he removed the screen and slid the window to the side. He jumped, pulling his body onto the sill and then rolling forward into the room.

The blind came off the wall with a loud crash, and he landed on the sharp edge of a piece of furniture.

The pain in his side was excruciating, but he was relieved to find no sign of blood. Slowly, he extricated himself from the blinds and set them aside. The house was still silent. He sat up and waited a few more minutes before he rose, went to the door, and cracked it. The hallway was dark, and appeared deserted. He slid out of the room.

A light hit him in the eyes just as he entered the hall. He looked down and noticed a red dot on his chest.

"Freeze zadrota," the accented voice of a girl called out.

He froze, knowing the voice. "Wait, I can explain," he mumbled. The dot wavered for a second and he thought she was really going to pull the trigger, but instead the hall lights came on.

They stood ten feet apart. "You break into a house like you

sail a boat. What a loser."

She motioned with the gun for him to move toward a large open space. Once they were in the living room, she waved the gun at a chair. Just as he sat, she came toward him. He flinched as the butt of the gun struck his face.

* * *

Dick was becoming more anxious with every mile as Kyle stayed right at the speed limit on the Crosstown Expressway. Finally they exited and headed toward Ybor City. The stress of the last few days had left his nerves frazzled. The bar they worked at was the best shot at scoring some weed, or maybe something stronger. Fourth Street was quiet this early in the week, and they quickly found a parking spot a block from the club.

They entered and moved to the side of the door so they could speak with the bouncer without blocking the entrance. Kyle was doing most of the talking, with Dick lurking nervously behind him. The man reached into his jacket pocket and subtly brought his hand around his back to meet Dick's waiting grasp. Dick moved further into the corner, opened the vial, and put a pill under his tongue. He motioned for Kyle to come closer, handed him a pill, and grinned as he put it in his mouth.

Now it was just a few beers and a matter of time until the drug took effect. Dick moved to the bar, looking forward to the next few hours. This was not the typical pot buzz, where he would have to worry about the effects wearing off quickly. What he assumed was ecstasy would carry him through the night.

The bar was full of regulars and employees on one of those rare nights when the right combination of people were there; the energy palpable. He moved toward the bar with Kyle behind him and ordered a beer. As the bartender came over, someone yelled from down the bar to put it on their tab.

On hearing this bit of good news, Dick quickly ordered two

double shots of tequila to supplement the beers and accelerate the effect of the drug. He collected the drinks, clinked glasses, with Kyle, downed the shot, and moved down the bar to greet his benefactor.

* * *

Greg paced the parking lot in front of the fish house. In the background, the sound of a saw pierced the quiet night. He wasn't too concerned about boat traffic this late, but he knew making this much noise after sundown was like a magnet for code enforcement, or worse, the police. Code enforcement would shut him down with either a stern warning or a ticket. His past transgressions, although they had never convicted him of anything, made the outcome less promising if it was the police that came by.

There was also the chance that Will would return, but that was the least of his worries. He was confident he could easily deal with the spineless contractor.

The grinding sound of the saw stopped and he leaned over to look under the building. Two men stood on the makeshift barge. James stood with a large circular saw held at his side, while the other man wobbled slightly, holding a light wherever James pointed. They moved five feet toward the edge of the building and the saw kicked on again. Greg rose and watched the traffic on Gulf Boulevard.

James had reported to him on the progress at the fish house. His knowledge of construction had quickly clued him in to how Will was planning on doing the work, but he needed one more day to see the entire process. He had explained that jacking up a building from the water and in sandy soil was not something he had ever done. There had to be a learning curve, and Will had already mastered it.

Greg hadn't understood much of what James had said, but as long as he was confident he could do it after watching Will, that

141

was good enough. He had made the quick decision that Will was now dispensable, and once he was out of the way, James's ability to finish the job would give him the upper hand with Lance. Until this point, Lance had run the operation like a dictator, treating him as a lowly fisherman. Now the tables would turn.

The saw paused again, and he looked anxiously at his phone. They had been at it for almost an hour now, and they needed to finish before Will returned. It was better to create an accident than to confront him directly, although that might be more satisfying.

Ten minutes later, he heard the two men unloading tools onto the seawall, and James called out that they were finished.

"You guys got it?" Greg asked as he walked toward them.

"It'll do the job. I just have to watch how he jacks up the building and sets the first beam. The spot we just cut is the next area. I'll make sure it looks like an accident."

* * *

"Dude, you on it yet?" Dick asked Kyle after another double tequila.

"Yeah, but this ain't X."

"Who cares? I'm feelin' it," Dick said as he moved down the bar to a cluster of women. The group parted to let him join them. The women were well dressed and having a good time. Dick looked out of place amongst the group, but they greeted him and started buying drinks. A few minutes later, he caught Kyle's eye down the bar and waved him over. Weeknights were more of a local crowd than the weekends, when the area was invaded by college students. The girls in the group were from South Tampa and had gone to school with them; the bonds formed in high school crossed any socio economic barriers. They were just all buddies out for a good time

Their group at the bar got rowdier as the night wore on. Dick had heard them talking about celebrating something, but he couldn't make out what it was. And he really didn't care. Whatever the bouncer had given them was bearing down on him full bore, and he couldn't have been happier.

The moment was broken when he felt someone grab his shirt from behind. He looked back and it was the bar owner pulling him away from the group.

"I told you not to mess with the customers, you low-life piece of crap. I saw you take that waitress out of here last night, too."

"Dickhead, bro. Wassup?" he slurred. "Come on, dude, lighten up. I'll hook you up with whichever of these fine women you want."

"You will get out of my bar now, and this will be the last time I see you unless it is across a courtroom. And take your sidekick with you!" he yelled in Dick's face.

Dick looked down, the high felt moments ago plummeting. "Dude, I'm just having some fun."

The man didn't answer, but looked at the bouncer and waved him over. He spoke in his ear when he approached and stepped out of the way. The bouncer closed in on Dick and pulled him away from the bar.

"Look. I gotta keep this gig. Sorry, bro," he whispered as he escorted him toward the door, looking behind him to make sure Kyle was following. They were outside now, and he handed Dick two more pills. "Don't worry about the other one, either. I like you guys. Sorry."

Dick popped both pills into his mouth.

"You did it this time!" Kyle yelled at him. "Now what? We got to pay Rucker off, and we got no money or job. Will has those other dudes now, and they at least show up on time."

Dick thought for a minute. "Dude, the fish. We go find the dude and spy him out. Find out where he's bringing the fish in and take another one."

"And how are we going to do that?"

"I don't know. I'm feeling a little Bondish right now."

"You idiot. That's not what you're feeling."

* * *

"So, it would be nice if you had my money and maybe I wouldn't have to turn you over to Gregori," Jazmyn said.

He had just regained consciousness and was looking around, trying to orient himself. Duct tape bound his ankles and wrists tightly to the chair, and his head was spinning again; the blow from the gun must have compounded his injuries from yesterday.

"I'll get your money. Just let the girl go," Will spat out as he frantically looked around him for a way out.

"The girl. I forgot about her." She turned away. "This could be fun."

Will couldn't help but watch her butt as she swayed across the room into the opposite hallway. A minute later she emerged, pushing Sheryl in front of her.

"Look what we have here," she said. "Your boyfriend here owes me ten thousand dollars for the other night. He doesn't seem to be able to pay me."

"What is she talking about, Will?" Sheryl asked.

"It's kind of involved," he said, regretting the way it came out the minute he opened his mouth.

"I bet it is. We're broken up for two days and you take on this Russian slut."

Jazmyn turned and looked at her, but was interrupted when the door to the garage opened and Greg entered. He looked around and laughed. "See you found her soft spot."

Chapter 20

Dick woke to sand flies feasting on his legs, and immediately sensed that the drugs had worn off. He sat up and brushed the invisible bugs off. They had driven to the beach last night without a plan; their scrambled brains assuring them of instant success.

It took him a few minutes to remember what they were supposed to be succeeding at. Finally it came back to him: All they had to do was find Greg and follow him to wherever he was stashing the fish now. It had seemed simpler last night. Now, in full daylight and sober, Dick realized it wasn't going to happen so easily.

A quick slap on Kyle's back stirred him. Another and he was awake.

"What the heck? Where are we?" He sat up and looked around.

"The beach, you idiot. Now get up. We need to figure some shit out." Dick got to his feet and started toward the parking area. He reached the pavement and brushed the sand from his bare legs and clothes. The car should have been right there, but it wasn't.

"Hurry up. Where'd you park, anyway?"

Kyle was slowly making his way toward him. "Fuck, Dick. It was right here." He walked up to a sign. "Tow-away zone. No overnight parking. Shit."

"Well, who told you to park there?" Dick walked toward him and stared at the sign they hadn't seen last night. "What are we going to do now?"

"We got no coin, no car, and no weed." Kyle checked his pants pockets. "And the phone was in the car. It's fucking dismal." He kicked the curb and then grabbed his foot in pain.

Dick looked around them. There was only one option—the fish house was a few blocks away. They hadn't been fired or quit — at least he didn't think so. He checked the level of the sun in the sky.

"It's still early. We can walk over to the fish house and just go to work." Surprised by his calmness without the benefit of weed, he smiled, knowing the drugs from last night, even though they had worn off, would temporarily change the chemistry in his brain.

He started walking toward Gulf Boulevard, where Kyle quickly caught up to him. The smell of food and coffee were hard to ignore as they passed a bakery and crossed the street to the intracoastal side. Two blocks later, they stood in front of the building.

"He's not even here yet," Kyle said as he checked the lock on the door.

Dick was checking the cooler out, on the off chance that Greg had used it again. The door was locked. He walked past it and onto the dock toward the sailboat. The cabin was locked from the outside.

* * *

The tires screeched as the truck made the turn too quickly and bounced into the lot. It came to a stop, one of the back doors opened, and Will was pushed onto the asphalt. Before he could get to his feet, the truck accelerated and sped out of the lot. He stayed on his knees, trying to evaluate his condition. His leg was bleeding through the rash of dark paving adhered to it from the fall, and his head still hurt.

Slowly, he got to his feet and staggered to the fish house.

"Hey."

He jumped and turned to the voice. Kyle and Dick stood in front of him, not looking much better than he felt. Realizing that he had walked right past them, he sat down on a pile of lumber on the floor and put his head in his hands.

It had been a long night. Greg had left him with Jazmyn and she had spent the night taunting him while he had returned Sheryl to the room she was being held in. Then he had gone to bed, leaving the two of them alone.

Jazmyn had been unrelenting for most of the night, claiming payback for the way he'd drugged her and taken her on the sailboat. Starting with a few blows to the body with the gun stock, she had swung from one personality to another, constantly keeping him off guard. One minute she was dancing for him, the next she pulled his belt off and whipped him with it. Finally, daylight changed the mood, and Greg appeared to break up the party.

"What the fuck? Can you leave something left of the guy? He's got to finish the building."

She turned. "I want my money and I'll leave him alone."

"Shit, bitch. I'll take it off your tab for bringing your crazy ass over here. All you girls seem to forget how much better things are here than where you came from. Don't forget those cold winters in Russia. Look around you, and think about what you're doing."

She cast one more nasty look at Will, lowered her head, and left the room.

Will tried to regain some sense of equilibrium now that she was gone. Greg had startled him back to the present. He got in his face and dictated the terms of his release. He was free to go as long as he finished the fish house. Sheryl would be released as soon as the job was complete. It was that easy, he said.

With his release imminent, he had decided not to question Greg's sincerity, just get out. Now he sat in the fish house, tired from a sleepless night, probably suffering from at least a concussion and his body ached every time he tried to move. He assumed he was being watched, so going to the police, even if they would listen, was out of the question. The only thing he could do was to get to work and hope Greg would keep his word.

"You guys are early," he said.

"Long story, but we're here for you." Kyle said.

Will looked at them and decided that as unreliable as they were, it was better to have someone in his confidence than no one. So he told them about Sheryl being abducted and Greg's terms. When he finished, they sat and stared at each other for several minutes, no one knowing what to say or do. The silence was broken when James came in.

"Where do you want to start boss?" He grinned at Will and patted him on the back. "You don't look so good."

Will ignored the comment and tried to concentrate on the job. "I want to set the first beam on the piles we installed yesterday." He knew James was either working for Greg or Lance, but he was competent and, although their means and motives differed, all involved wanted the building finished.

James nodded. "You working the underside again?"

"Yeah, I'll take the boys down with me. You and the other guys can work from the top." He got up slowly. "Why don't you measure the beam and get it cut? I'll show these guys what to do below."

He walked toward the door, went to the seawall, and untied the raft. Dick and Kyle followed him onto it, and he pulled it toward the two piles they had set. Once there, he hooked his tape measure over one, measured the distance between them, and called the measurement up to James. A few minutes later, he heard the saw bite through wood, and then one end of the beam appeared through the hole.

Will supervised while Dick and Kyle set up the jacks. Kyle worked in the water, setting the steel plates to keep the posts from driving into the ground when pressure was applied, and Dick worked above, setting the jack and the post up to the old floor beam. Once the shoring was straight and plumb, Will started cranking the jack to put pressure on the old floor, slowly raising it a few inches.

With the extra space they had created, the beam slid easily into place. The jacks were lowered and the building settled onto the new supports. All three quickly nailed everything together, and the section was complete. He was happy with the progress. With the extra help, it had taken less than an hour to set the beam— something that might have taken the entire day with just the three of them. He pulled the raft toward the seawall and they got off.

"Take a break for a few," he said to Dick and Kyle as he went to the building to talk to James.

Inside, he bounced on the section of floor they had just reinforced.

"It's tight. That went pretty smooth. We can send the poles down to you if you want to start the new holes," James said.

"Give me a few. Cut them at fourteen feet and drill the tops like we did the other ones. I'll get suited up and jet them in." A hopeful energy had taken the place of the fatigue he had felt earlier, the progress on the building gave him some hope. Even though Sheryl was still in danger, it was exhilarating to do something people said was impossible and hopefully free her in the process.

He went to the seawall and started gearing up, giving instructions to Dick and Kyle as he readied himself for the next phase. "Go on up and help him rotate the pile when I start to jet it."

He pushed the platform into place, tied it off, and called up that he was ready. The pole slid through the hole and penetrated the water. As soon as he was sure it was resting on the bottom, he called up for the jet rig. They passed him the iron pipe, attached to a hose fed through the hole.

"Turn on the pump. I'm going in," he yelled up, and slid off the raft.

Water shot from the one-inch pipe, moving the sand and small rocks out of the way. The pole sank deeper with every turn. Soon it hit bedrock, and they started on the next one. It was lunchtime when he emerged from the water. Dick, Kyle, and James met him at the seawall and helped with the gear.

"I gotta take a break," he said, shivering. The hours in the water even with the wetsuit had chilled him.

"No problem. I can cut the poles and get the beam ready," James said.

Will went to the sailboat and climbed aboard. He unlocked the cabin and took a jug of water and the leftover snook onto the deck, where he sat in the sun. If he could get the beam set this afternoon, he would go back to Greg and demand Sheryl's release. He finished the food and walked back to the job. James had the poles cut and the beam ready to go.

"I'll go below and get the jacks set," Will said as he looked around for Dick and Kyle. "Where'd the boys go?"

"Got me. They said they were going to get some food. That's all I know."

"Oh well, hopefully they'll be back when we're ready to set the beam." He turned and went to the platform, checked the equipment on the plywood deck, and pulled himself underneath. With the jacks set up, he started to go from one to the other, taking a little more pressure with each crank. The building groaned as it started to lift—a part of the process that sent chills through him.

But he knew if he kept the pressure equal it would work.

Slowly, the building lifted one inch, and then two. He was

just about to take the final inch on the first pile when he heard something bump the raft. He fell in the water, his body smashing against one of the temporary poles on his way in.

* * *

Dick opened his eyes and turned to Kyle as the building shook above him. He and Kyle were on the lower deck, facing the intracoastal used for unloading fish from the boats before being hoisted above. They had no lunch money so they had taken two of Will's fishing rigs and were hand lining small snapper. Both had soon fallen asleep.

"Shit." Kyle dove into the water. "Come on, Dick. Will's in there."

Dick followed him into the water, and they swam toward the platform. But Will was nowhere to be seen.

"Stay here and watch for him," Kyle said as he climbed on the raft.

Dick looked behind him, feeling something before he saw it. A dorsal fin pierced the surface, and he scrambled for the raft.

"It's a shark!" Kyle yelled, pointing at it. "It must have been feeding on the tuna carcass."

Dick was searching the water for Will. "I don't see him."

Will's head broke the surface ten feet from the boat, and he gasped at them, "The jet!"

The boys looked at each other as they watched the fin circle between Will and the platform.

"The jet!" he yelled again.

Kyle caught on and grabbed the pipe they had been using to jet the holes. He turned the valve on and water shot from the end. Directing the spray at the shark, he watched as it became disoriented and stopped swimming.

Dick helped Will onto the platform as Kyle kept the spray of water on the shark, and as soon as he was onboard, they started frantically pulling themselves to the seawall. He looked down at Will who was passed out next to him.

"Dude's had a rough day. Let's get him inside."

The roar of an engine going too fast through the no-wake zone startled the boys before rocking the raft with its wake.

"That's that prick Greg," Kyle said as they moved Will onto solid ground. Both boys turned to look, and couldn't help but notice Sheryl's auburn hair as the boat cruised past.

Chapter 21

Will sat up and looked around, unsure where he was or how he had gotten here. The dim interior of the fish house slowly came into focus as his eyes adjusted to the light. He was soaking wet and remembered a loud noise and then going in the water.

"What happened? How long was I out?"

Dick and Kyle fumbled over each other to tell the story.

"And you saw Greg heading out the pass?" Will asked when they were done.

"Yeah. Dude was flying through the no-wake zone. Couldn't miss him," Dick said.

Will's brain was close to fully functioning now. "Anyone with him?"

"I think he had Sheryl," Kyle said.

He thought for a second, "Lance keeps his boat next door. One of you go over and ask them to put it in the water. Tell them that he asked you to do some work on it. I'm going below to see what happened. Then we're going after them. He's only got a few minutes headstart."

Will wanted to check the damage below to confirm his suspicions that sabotage had taken place. He could easily check it out by the time Lance's boat would be in the water. As he pulled the raft under the building he realized that if it hadn't been for the shark, he would have taken another crank on the jacks and been right below the beam when it fell. James was nowhere in sight, so he had been right, that he was a ringer sent in by Lance or Greg, to see how the work was being done. They must have booby trapped the site after he'd figured it out, to get rid of him.

It all made sense now, but he had been so happy to have competent help that he'd overlooked the signs.

If the beam had been cut and did not break, he knew they were trying to kill him, and that Sheryl awaited the same fate aboard Greg's boat.

The boys decided that Kyle would go next door, leaving Dick to go underneath the building with Will. They went back to the platform and pushed their way under the building. When they reached the area that had fallen, it was obvious to Will that the beam had been cut. The saw marks were fresh, unweathered like the rest of the wood. If the boys had not been there, he was sure he would be dead.

As they pulled out of the shadows, they could see Lance's boat gleaming in the sun as the forklift lowered it into the water. Kyle waited while the operator slid the forks out, took the bow, and held it by the seawall. Will and Dick were quickly by his side.

"He says the keys are in it," Kyle said.

"Good work. I have to go to the sailboat and grab some things. You guys walk it down the dock toward the end. I'll meet you there."

He took off down the dock and hopped onto the sailboat. Inside the cabin, he opened the chart table and pulled out the GPS. In seconds he was back on the dock, moving toward Lance's boat.

They jumped down to the deck and Will got behind the wheel. He started the blower to evacuate any gas fumes from the engine compartment that could be ignited from a spark when the engine started. After a long thirty seconds, he turned the key. The large stern drive engine roared to life, and he wasted no time letting it warm up. He pushed off the dock and eased the left handle forward. The transmission clicked into forward and he pushed down the right lever. With a jerk, the boat jumped from the dock, almost pulling the wheel from his hands. A quick glance showed the trim tabs were out of alignment. He adjusted the port side and the boat straightened out.

In minutes, they were past Sand Key and into the open Gulf. Will glanced at the rpm gauge, which was pegged right at the red zone, and backed off the speed slightly. It would do no good to blow the engine. The needle dropped into the green and he glanced at the speedometer. At forty knots, the Middle Grounds were only two hours away.

"Hey, Kyle. Take the wheel for a minute," he yelled over the engine. Kyle shot him a *who me* look, but tentatively moved toward him. Will kept a hold on the helm until he was sure Kyle had a grip on it. Letting the wheel loose at this speed could result in the boat turning sharply and possibly flipping.

As he moved out of the way, he yelled in Kyle's ear, "Just keep the same course!"

He stepped aside and watched as the boy got the feel for the boat. A smile soon crossed Kyle's worried face, and Will turned toward the GPS. The started up and he waited as it acquired the satellites necessary to calculate their position. After several minutes, the screen changed and showed their location, bearing, and speed.

He sat down on the bench seat and started to scroll through the screens, finally settling on the waypoint page. There he pressed one that he remembered as being in the cluster he had plotted several nights ago, and waited as the computer calculated the course. The bearing said 285, and he glanced at the compass mounted by the wheel.

Then he stood up and took the wheel from Kyle, moving it to the right and waiting as the boat changed course. When it settled at

285, he showed Kyle the compass and told him to hold the course.

There was no need to drive as long as Kyle could hold the bearing and speed. The Gulf was wide open and obstruction free, unlike the Keys, where you had to know the waters to avoid the shallows and shoals. He glanced over to check the course, and looked at the other instruments. A digital depth finder showed the bottom to be thirty feet under the hull. It would gradually deepen from here — no need to worry about shallow water. With the GPS showing the boat arriving at the waypoint in seventy-five minutes, he sat down to figure out what to do when they found them.

He figured Greg would run close to the course they were on. Just as he went to check the GPS again, he saw a boat on the horizon. It was too far away to know for sure, but the profile was similar to Greg's.

He took the wheel from Kyle, eased the throttle slightly, and changed course for the boat. As they closed the distance, he had no doubt it was Greg's. But what was he doing here? This was miles from the Middle Grounds and the bluefin water he fished.

He slowed even more, veering off the collision course they were on. It would do no good to threaten him before he could come up with a plan. The details on the boat soon became visible. Two figures, one of them surely Greg, were huddled at the transom, staring at one of the engines tilted out of the water. Will suspected they had entangled the prop in some debris, or were having engine trouble, and the boat was drifting.

Sheryl was not visible, and he moved closer as he searched the deck for her. The men saw him approach.

They started to wave him over and it took him a minute to figure out that they thought he was Lance. With an excuse to close the gap further, he idled toward the drifting boat, only wanting to get close enough to see if Sheryl was there.

"Get down!" he called to Kyle and Dick. "I don't want him to see anyone with me." He started to circle the boat. With each pass, he closed the gap. She was still nowhere to be seen, but he was close enough to see the bare shaft on the lower unit of the engine. They had lost a propeller and he remembered Kyle's story of untangling the fishing line. Somehow in the process the cotter pin must have come loose. The boat was crippled, not able to reach anywhere near its top speed with only one engine. Twin outboards were synced together, their propellers opposing each other to make the boat run true. With only one engine, Greg would only be able to make fifteen knots, and have to fight the wheel the whole time to hold course. Will could easily keep an eye on the boat until the authorities arrived.

"What the fuck are you doing?"

Will heard the scream from Greg across the fifty yards separating them. "Where's Sheryl?" he screamed back.

"You mean that bitch of yours? She's right here." Greg leaned into the cabin and came back with his hand full of auburn hair. Sheryl was forced onto the deck. "Here she is. What are you going to do about it?"

Will was shocked speechless. He looked around the well-appointed cockpit, but there was nothing close to resembling a weapon. "Check the cabin. See if there is anything down there," he said to Kyle.

Kyle reappeared and shook his head.

Will reached into his pocket and pulled out his cell phone, planning on circling the crippled boat to keep him here until help could arrive. But the screen showed no service, which meant he would have to get closer to shore. With Greg's limited speed and decreased maneuverability, he should have the advantage, and started to move back and forth on the seaward side of the boat.

Greg went to the helm. The maneuver was forcing him to move or risk a possible collision of which Lance's larger boat would be the winner. Will moved closer with each pass until Greg started the remaining motor and turned to shore. He felt like a sheepdog pushing his flock ahead of him as he crisscrossed Greg's wake, moving the slower boat in the direction he wanted. The shoreline soon became visible, and Will thought about his options.

They would lose their advantage in the close quarters of the pass, and Greg knew those waters better. If he took Bunces Pass into Boga Ciega Bay, he could easily lose him. With his hand shielding his eyes, he scanned the beach, settling on a large pink building. The Don Cesar hotel was the most expensive and exclusive place on the beach, having housed everyone from rock stars to presidents. It was also the best landmark.

With a few adjustments, he soon had Greg moving toward the building. Now it was time to get the police involved. He picked up the phone, hoping he had service now, and dialed 911. The reception was crystal clear when the operator answered. After explaining his situation, he had the operator confirm his number. She said that someone would call him right back. He put the phone on the dashboard so he could see it if a call came through, and continued his course.

They were in green water, now, no more than a quarter-mile from the beach, when something jarred the boat. Will had been so intent on Greg's boat that he had not seen the speed boat pulling a para-sailer off the beach. The wake threw him off balance, and he was unable to catch the phone as it slid off the polished dashboard and landed on the deck. Once past the wake, he leaned over to pick it up, but the screen was shattered and it would not respond. With no way for the police to contact him, he threw the phone down and focused on Greg.

His best chance was to drive him onto the beach and force a confrontation. If Greg had a gun, he figured he would have used it already. Will had the boys, so they outnumbered Greg and his deckhand. What he hoped was that Greg would hit the beach and run, leaving Sheryl on the boat. As they approached the beach, the para-sail boat cut between them, allowing Greg a large buffer.

The fishing boat hit the beach and he watched as Greg pulled Sheryl out and headed toward the Don Cesar. Swimmers scattered as Will plowed the hull of the larger boat onto the beach, but by the time he was off the boat, Greg and Sheryl had disappeared. He looked back, saw Dick and Kyle following behind him, and took off toward the building.

Angry tourists huddled under blue umbrellas, screamed at them as they kicked sand at them, but they didn't slow down. They scaled the wide limestone stairs three at a time, and were quickly on the pool deck. Will saw Greg push past a cocktail waitress and enter the building. He skirted the pool and went for the door. The cool air and slick marble greeted him as he entered the building, and he slid several feet before gaining his balance, then ran straight through the lobby to the entrance.

Chapter 22

Lance leaned forward at his desk, staring intently at the computer screen. The red dot on the nautical chart was his boat, and it was moving quickly toward the beach. His key fob was clenched in his hand. The device automatically triggered an alarm that went to his phone whenever the fob was not in close proximity and the boat was moving. He had immediately called the marina when the app alerted him, and they described the three men that had taken it.

It had to be Will and those two troublemakers he had working for him. Greg had called earlier, saying that he was going out fishing, and that he could expect him back the next day, hopefully with a couple of bluefins, and minus one problem. That would take care of the girl, at least.

Surprised that Will had actually taken action, he wondered what his next move should be. Self preservation was always his priority, and he thought about sacrificing Greg to cover his involvement. The guy was a loose cannon, but he was also his biggest producer. Cut him out of the chain and it could cost him forty to fifty grand a week in season.

And finding a replacement that he could trust would not be easy.

Most fisherman, especially those open to working the black

market, were not the sharpest hooks in the tackle box. Greg was both shrewd and a talented fisherman, but his behavior, governed by his greed, was out of control. And it would lead right back to him if he was caught.

The dot on the screen was motionless now, hovering in front of the Don Cesar hotel. He watched it for another and made up his mind.

He picked up the phone and dialed.

"Brice here," the Fish and Game officer answered.

"Hey, it's Lance, from the fish house over in Pinellas."

"What can I do for you, Mr. Baitman?"

Lance called in several leads each year, mostly to sabotage his competition. His company also donated to several charities that benefited the Fish and Game officers, to stay in their favor.

"Got a lead on a poacher for you. Big bluefin tuna guy. He tried to sell to me last week. I bought one just to keep him on the hook. I expect to see him this afternoon." He admitted to the buy to cover his tracks if the officer started asking questions about activity in the fish house.

"Well done. I can get you reimbursed for the fish if this pans out. Let me know when he calls."

Lance disconnected and planned his next move. Greg's cell phone went right to voicemail. He assumed he was either out of range or unable to hear the ring over the engine noise. There was nothing further to be gained by sitting here watching a dot on a screen, so he shut down the computer and left his office, telling the secretary that he would be gone for the day. As he walked downstairs to the SUV, he looked up at the sky — a rain storm was imminent

Inside the car, the air conditioning cut through the humid air, and he turned on his iPad. Opening the same app he had viewed on his computer, he saw the dot was still in the same place. From the parking lot he crossed the railroad tracks again, cursing the advent of air freight. His family had bought the building back in the seventies, before Federal Express started overnighting fish anywhere in the world. Back then, it was important to be by the tracks. Now it cost double the freight to get fish to and from the landlocked building.

A few blocks later, he turned onto US 19 and headed south. A right on 54th Street took him over several causeways toward the beach. Traffic was heavy, and he tapped the steering wheel anxiously, watching the iPad screen as he waited. Finally he reached the beach, turned left, and made a quick right into the hotel's parking lot. He drove to the valet attendant, left the engine running, and ran up the steps to the lobby.

Out of breath by the time he reached the pool deck, he scanned the beach. His boat was pulled up on the sand, apparently unharmed. Greg's boat was off to the side.

He ran to the beach, slogging through the sand in his shoes. He winced as he went knee deep into the water before he could roll over the gunwale. Soaked from the waist down, he moved to the helm and checked the ignition. The key was still there. The engine started right away, and he hit the blower switch, knowing he was lucky not to have blown up the boat.

He closed his eyes and tried to steady his nerves. Too much could go wrong in the coming hours for him to make a mistake like that. Refocused, he looked toward the stern and put the engine in reverse. Not knowing if the stern drive was wrecked from grounding it in the sand, he pushed the throttle, hoping it would move.

The boat didn't react. Cursing, he gave it more gas and waited as the hull started to vibrate underneath him. Soon it pulled free, spitting a swath of sand in its wake. He drove carefully out of the swim area. Too many people knew him here to disregard common courtesy. Once clear, he turned south and pushed the throttle until the boat got up on plane. Five minutes later, he rounded the point and turned into the channel. He slowed the boat and pulled out his phone.

* * *

Greg pulled the phone from his pocket and looked at the caller ID. With a grimace he answered and listened. After a long minute he said, "Yes," and hung up.

He sat on the couch in his living room, shirt unbuttoned to his waist, sweating profusely and breathing like Darth Vader. Sheryl sat across from him, unrestrained. She could run if she wanted, but the shotgun leaning next to him discouraged her, although he doubted he could even raise it to fire at her in his current condition. He certainly couldn't chase her down.

Lance had been clear that this needed to end now. Now he had to decide what to do. Although he didn't like it, Lance was his meal ticket. He got up and looked at Sheryl.

"Jazmyn!" he yelled.

The girl came into the room.

"Watch our friend here. I'll be back," he said, handing her the shotgun.

* * *

Will paced the floor of the fish house. "What do we do now?"

"*We*? I don't see any we here," Dick said.

"Shut up, Dick." Kyle smacked him. "We need to get Sheryl back. You can't just walk away from this like everything else that goes wrong in your life."

Dick turned and walked outside.

"Let him go," Will said as he sat down on a pile of lumber. He had been dizzy since they hit the beach and the mile-long run from the Don Cesar hadn't helped. Greg had escaped and had probably taken Sheryl back to his house. He knew from the night before that going in there without a plan and something to back it up with was going to end badly.

"You don't look so good," Kyle said, handing him a jug of water.

"I'll be okay. Just have to think." Will sat there staring into space. The water helped, and he realized he was probably dehydrated; not the brightest thing to do with a concussion. His thoughts came back into focus, but he didn't trust his body yet. Even though his mind seemed to be working better, a plan eluded him. Going into Greg's backyard was not an option without reinforcements and weapons, neither of which he had. He was close to panic when Dick came running back inside.

"Law's here," he yelled, as he dropped through one of the holes in the floor.

Will heard the water splash just as he heard a knock and saw a silhouette standing in the doorway. "Can I help you?" he called out from where he sat.

"Fish and Game. Name's Brice." The man held out credentials.

Not sure where this was going, but with little choice, Will invited him in. The officer walked over to him and extended his hand. Will thought about getting up, but lacked the energy. He held his hand out and shook the man's hand.

"My name's Will. This is Kyle. I'm the contractor on the job here. What can we do for you?"

"I got a report of some poaching. Some guy is supposedly using the cooler outside as a drop point. You have a key?"

"No, the owner says he leases it to a guy named Greg." Will had no idea where this was going, and decided to offer little information.

"Mind if I look around?" the officer asked.

"Sure. Go ahead," Will said. Kyle was by one of the holes

and Will saw the blood on the floor from the other night when they had cut up the fish and hoisted it through the opening. Brice was looking out over the water, glancing down at the dock when Will had an idea.

"Kyle, we need to cover the holes so no one falls through. You want to grab a sheet of plywood and start with that one?" He pointed to the blood-stained area, hoping the four-by-eight sheet of wood would hide the stain.

Kyle went for the wood, but it was too late; they had attracted Brice's attention, and he started toward them. He was a dozen steps away, the blood just becoming visible, when they heard a boat pull up to the dock outside.

All three turned as a man yelled, "Can you toss me a line?"

Will struggled to his feet and went to the end of the building adjacent to the intracoastal. The officer was a step ahead, giving him the time to motion to Kyle to stay where he was and finish covering the hole. When he reached the window, he saw Lance idling by the low docks, waiting for a line to tie up.

"Better go around to the marina and tie up there," Will yelled. "There's no easy way in from there."

He turned toward the door and nodded to Kyle, who had just gotten the plywood into place. Brice followed him out the door and they went across to the marina and entered the pier running parallel to the building. Lance was just pulling up to an empty slip. Will stayed on the seawall and watched an employee run to help him tie off.

He waited where he was, watching Brice and Lance talking by the boat. They finished their conversation and came toward him. Not sure whether he should just put his hands out and await handcuffs, he stood stiffly.

"Officer has some questions about Greg," Lance said as he approached. "Why don't you help him out?" He lowered his voice, "Tell him the right story and we can still make this work."

Will picked up on the nuance and wondered what Lance was up to. He appeared to be throwing Greg under the bus. The law going after Greg might help get Sheryl back, so he went toward Brice. "Happy to help," he said.

Brice took out a notepad and asked Will for his personal information. Just as he was about to ask his first question, they heard the roar of a diesel engine pull into the parking lot. Both men turned simultaneously and watched as the black truck stopped and Greg got out. Will stared at the tinted windows to see if Sheryl was with him, but they were too dark.

Greg took one look at the officer and went for Lance. "What did you say?"

"Officer has some questions for you," Lance answered.

Will could see the panic in Lance's eyes as he waited to see what Greg would do. It took a few seconds for the larger man to react before he went for him.

"Bastard!" He pushed Lance into the water. He was caught by surprise and hit hard, but soon surfaced and swam to the closest pier.

"Goddamnit! I go down, I'm taking your sorry ass with me!" Lance yelled as he clung to the pole and tried to hoist himself onto the dock. It was low tide, and his hand fell inches short. He clung to the barnacle encrusted pile his arms dripping blood.

Brice stood next to Will, both men watching the action. Finally he turned to Will. "Can you please tell me what's going on here?"

"I'll tell you," the accented voice of a woman yelled.

Will looked over and saw Jazmyn standing in the bow of Greg's boat, a line in her hand. He looked toward the helm, and there was Sheryl at the wheel pulling up to the lower dock of the fish house.

"Bitch, stay out of this!" Greg yelled and stamped toward the building.

Just as Will and Brice entered the building, they saw him about to pass through the opening to the lower deck and confront her.

"Better watch what comes out of that mouth of yours!" Greg yelled at her.

Brice drew his gun. "Enough. No one move!"

Chapter 23

Will stood next to the officer, wondering what the two women were doing here, and apparently working together. Brice had the gun aimed at Greg, who eased himself away from the boat and moved toward the opening. Turning with a grace that belied his body, Greg drew a gun from his waistband and fired. Brice fell to the floor, grabbing his leg. Will froze, and watched as Greg made his way across the room. He looked down at Brice and watched as blood poured from the wound. The fallen officer reached for the microphone clipped to his lapel in an effort to call for help.

Before his hand reached it, Greg kicked his gun away and yanked at the wire connecting the microphone to the unit on his belt, then removed the radio and threw it into the water. Weaponless and unable to communicate, Brice rolled away from him and with his back against the wall he tried to stem the bleeding. Will was about to assist him when Greg went to a window opening overlooking the water.

He braced his elbows on the sill, extended the gun through the opening, and fired.

"Gregori!" he heard a woman scream.

"Both of you. In here now." He backed away to keep an eye on the room, but kept the gun aimed at the women as they tied off the boat.

"I want my money from the American and to be done with you. Bastard, threatening to send me back to Russia," Jazmyn spat at him.

Greg smiled as if he was enjoying himself. "When I'm done with you, you'll be back in the home country digging potatoes from the frozen ground on that piece of dirt I found you on."

Will rose and looked over at Sheryl, who seemed unharmed. He mouthed from an adjacent window, *are you ok?* She nodded back, a tear falling down her cheek. He was so intent on her that he didn't notice the movement out of the corner of his eye until it was too late. He had forgotten about the boy.

Kyle went for the gun Greg had kicked away from Brice's reach, but he was too slow, and Greg spun toward him. "Back away, sonny. I've had enough of all of you." He focused his aim on Sheryl. "Seems you're all attached to the girl here."

"Dude!" They heard a voice yell from below.

Kyle backed away from the gun, took a step toward an open hole, and jumped. Will knew it was now or never, and ran for Greg, who had turned to watch Kyle disappear. Before he reached him, he stumbled and lost his balance, careening into the bigger man. His momentum carried Greg forward a few feet, and they landed on the plywood sheet.

The wood splintered and Greg fell through the hole, pulling Will with him. He hit the water, barely missing the beam they had just installed. Somehow Greg had fit through the opening and was swimming for the boat. Will reached out for him, but he was just past his grasp.

Again the larger man showed his athletic prowess. He was already at Lance's boat, trying to climb the swim ladder and fighting off the two women. Their fists raining down on him had no visible effect and with a loud grunt, he pulled himself aboard. Swinging his arms like a bear, he knocked each of them to the deck and went to the helm.

Will heard the boat start and knew he had to do something, and now. He was just past the last piling, still a dozen feet from the boat when he saw Greg take aim at Lance. With a grin on his face, he pulled the throttle back and moved toward the piling.

It was too late and a loud scream came from Lance's mouth as the propellor tore into his legs. He tried to scramble up the piling, but fell into the water. Will could only watch the stream of red drift back from the propellor. Greg pushed the throttle forward and eased away from the carnage with a big grin on his face. The two women were huddled against the transom.

Will swam away from the building. His only chance was to show himself and act as bait and lure Greg into making a mistake. He swam back to the building and yelled for Greg, The predator saw its prey and the boat came toward him. Waiting until the last minute, Sheryl's scream was the last thing he heard as the shadow from the hull screened him from Greg. Taking a huge breath, he dove into the murky waters and pulled for the bottom. He needed to get deep, and fast before the propellor hit him.

He grabbed the piling and had an idea. The pry bar he had been using when the accident had happened the other day had never been recovered. If he could find it, he could jamb it into the propellor and disable the boat before Greg made a run for it. Once the boat was out of sight, he feared he would never see Sheryl again.

Moving to the next row of pilings, he surfaced for a second to take another breath. He had heard the boat's engine while underwater, but it was impossible to tell direction and he had no idea what they were doing. After a deep inhale, he looked through the shadows of the building and saw the boat circling, obviously looking for him. He released the breath and took another, then pulled himself underwater. There was no time to waste.

On the bottom now, he tried to assemble a picture of what had happened above him yesterday. Slowly the scene came back to him and he watched himself fall. In slow motion, he watched the pry bar leave his hand and drop in the water. If he was right, it should be just a few feet in front of him. Leaving the piling, he clawed across the sandy bottom, wedging his fingers into the muck to hold him down. If he released the grip, he would float to the surface.

The receptors deep in his lungs screamed for oxygen and he felt a burning sensation as they found only carbon dioxide. A convulsion overtook him and he almost gagged. If he didn't find the bar in the next few seconds he would have to surface again. Reaching out ahead for another handhold, his fingers brushed something that felt like metal. He grabbed it and pushed off the bottom.

His head broke the surface and he gasped for air. After a quick breath he turned to the intracoastal. The boat was still there, but moving farther away. It would just take a small push of the throttles to take Sheryl away from him.

He kicked toward open water, using his one free hand to help his legs. The boat was about fifty feet away now. So far he had been unobserved and he made a last push toward the transom, needing just a few more seconds to reach it. Just when the engine was within striking distance, the boat started to turn its bow towards the inlet. Will expected him to accelerate and take off for open water, either shredding him, or leaving him behind. Neither was an acceptable outcome.

He could feel the prop wash push against him as he closed on the boat. With a last effort he lunged forward, thrusting the pry bar in front of him. The sound of the engine vibrated through his head and bubbles surrounded him, making it impossible to see. The first thrust met no resistance and he pulled the bar back for another attempt. Just as he did, he could feel the vibration of the propellor change and like a sonar beacon, he knew where to strike. Pushing the bar forward again, he felt resistance and the torque of the propellor as it tried to pull the bar out of his hands.

With both hands, he fought it. Greg must have felt something, because the RPMs increased suddenly, almost tearing the bar from his hands. But he had to hang on. Feeling his grip weaken, he shoved the steel bar forward one more time and let the propellor take it.

There was nothing left to do but drop back and wait. The pitch of the engine changed and he knew it had worked.

Now, the question was how to get Sheryl. He looked up at the boat and saw it idling away. He was not too worried about losing it now. If Greg tried to make a run, the engine would blow in a matter of minutes. Looking around he saw the marina dock only feet away and the transom of his sailboat several slips in. With a few hard kicks he reached it and climbed aboard. Running forward, he released the lines, not worrying now what damage the wind or tides would do to the hull, and quickly went to the transom where he yanked on the starter cord.

The engine sputtered but wouldn't start. He tried again and this time breathed in relief as it turned over. With the tiller in hand, he set the lever in reverse and backed out of the slip.

Shifting into forward, the boat cleared the dock and he was in open water, the power boat only a few hundred feet ahead of him now. Greg was at the transom, staring into the water, trying to find the problem. This gave Will the opportunity he needed and he gunned the small engine, heading directly toward Lance's boat.

It was almost too late when he realized he hadn't accounted for Greg's gun. The big man saw him coming, pulled it from his waistband and aimed directly at him. Instinctively Will ducked, hitting his head on the boom as he dodged the bullet. The force of the strike must have released the vang, and the aluminum spar swung up, leaving him exposed, but also giving him an idea. He moved forward, reached for the main sheet and released the lock holding the line. The boom was free now.

With a push on the tiller he angled the sailboat toward the powerboat and moved back to the helm, releasing all the line. With his arms around the boom, he waited. Greg aimed and fired again when he saw the boat approaching, but he didn't see what was coming at him until it was too late. Just as the two boats came alongside each other, Will pushed off the deck as hard as he could, clinging to the boom as it swung across the three feet of open water and crashed into Greg, throwing him off his feet.

Before Will could regain his balance, he heard another shot. Looking down at the deck, he saw a pool of blood and for one uncertain second, thought it was his, until the boom swung another foot forward and he saw Greg prone with blood pooling around his head. Jazmyn stood over him with the gun. Will jumped off the boom, landing off balance on the deck and saw the barrel swing over to him.

"Drop the weapon, now!" a voice came across the water.

Jazmyn lowered the gun, but did not drop it. She looked at Will. "He is dead. Now you owe me." She dropped the gun and placed her hands above her head.

Minutes later, two sheriff's deputies were aboard. One secured the two boats together. The other took Jazmyn across to their boat, then handcuffed her to the rail. Will and Sheryl were ordered to board the sheriff's boat.

It took a good half hour to explain what had just happened, but finally, they seemed satisfied and let Sheryl and Will go.

Just as they were about to board the sailboat, Sheryl looked over at Jazmyn. "Don't worry. We will help you."

The Russian looked back at her and winked.

Epilogue

The boat cut through the two-foot swell as Will lashed the tiller and trimmed the sails. He sat back and watched the waves. It had taken two days for the police to tell him he was no longer suspected of anything, and he knew that Brice's account had helped things considerably. Somehow he had made it to the marina and called the sheriff.

Sheryl had stayed on the sailboat with him in the meantime, some of their former closeness returning. It wasn't the throws of passion, as it had been, but it was more than he knew he should expect.

She'd explained how Jazmyn had colluded with her after Greg had threatened her and stormed out of the house. The threat of Greg returning her to Russia had forced her to choose sides. The two women had reached an uneasy peace.

Will had told the whole story of meeting Jazmyn in the bar, drugging her, and the rescue at sea the next day.

"I can't go back to work at the club. Not after all this. And we still don't know what happened to Dick and Kyle," she said.

"I think they're okay. The foam platform was missing and I suspect they Huck Finned it down the intracoastal. Those guys are like cats, they'll land on their feet."

"I hope so. I really did like them." She paused. "I don't want to ask you what you're going to do with your life like an ultimatum, but I have to know what you're thinking."

Will took a deep breath. "Lance's daughter came by this morning when you were still asleep. The family is committed to finishing the fish house and turning it into a restaurant. They want to sell the old processing building and get out of the fish business."

"Where does that leave you?"

"They want me to continue the work. She paid me up to date and said I could start back as soon as the police cleared the building as a crime scene." He looked over the side.

"But?"

"But I need to get my license reinstated and do this legally." He frowned.

"You know, we could do this together. I still want to go to school, but I can help do the office work." She looked away.

"But?"

"But this boat's gotta go."

He leaned across the cockpit and kissed her. "Yeah, it's got bad karma anyway, Partner."

Thanks For Reading

If you liked the book please leave a review:
Leave a Review Here

For more information please check out my web page:
https://stevenbeckerauthor.com/

Or follow me on Facebook:
https://www.facebook.com/stevenbecker.books/

Made in United States
Troutdale, OR
12/14/2023

15853068R00108